She fumbled for the bolt behind her and pulled it back, keeping her eyes on Evan all the while.

"I'm going home now. I think it's best if we try to forget what just happened and keep things as they were. You tend to your other businesses, and I'll run the restaurant. I'll keep you informed about anything you need to know, but the less we have to see each other, the better."

Evan only stared at her, his eyes taking on the hue of dark thunderclouds. More shaken than she wanted to admit, Jenny let herself out of the restaurant and hurried home.

She bolted her door behind her and managed to cross the room to the sofa before her tottery legs gave out. Sinking back against the cushion, she dug her fingers into the upholstery and looked around at the room she had decorated with such care. Where was the security she once felt within these walls?

Gone, she realized. Dissipated like a puff of smoke after Evan's advances. She trembled again, but this time in anger instead of fear. Back in Prescott, he had offered her a business opportunity and a new life, a chance at a new beginning. How dare he ruin it with his disgusting overtures?

Jenny dropped her forehead onto her knees, her anger giving way to despair. Had she traveled all this distance to escape her past only to find herself enmeshed in the same kind of vile trap. . .with no one to come to her rescue this time?

**CAROL COX** is a native of Arizona whose time is devoted to being a pastor's wife, keeping up with her college-age son's schedule, home-schooling her young daughter, and serving as a church pianist, youth worker, and 4-H leader. She loves any activity she can share with her family in addition to her own pursuits in reading, crafts, and local history. She also has had several novels and novellas published. Carol and her family make their home in northern Arizona.

Books by Carol Cox

**HEARTSONG PRESENTS**
HP264—Journey Toward Home
HP344—The Measure of a Man
HP452—Season of Hope
HP479—Cross My Heart
HP580—Land of Promise

Don't miss out on any of our super romances. Write to us at the following address for information on our newest releases and club information.

Heartsong Presents Readers' Service
PO Box 721
Uhrichsville, OH 44683

Or check out our Web site at www.heartsongpresents.com

# Refining Fire

*Carol Cox*

Heartsong Presents

*To Dave,*
*Now and always*

**A note from the Author:**
*I love to hear from my readers! You may correspond with me by writing:*

> **Carol Cox**
> **Author Relations**
> **PO Box 719**
> **Uhrichsville, OH 44683**

**ISBN 1-59310-097-3**

**REFINING FIRE**

All Scripture quotations are taken from the King James Version of the Bible.

*Our mission is to publish and distribute inspirational products offering exceptional value and biblical encouragement to the masses.*

All of the characters and events in this book are fictitious. Any resemblance to actual persons, living or dead, or to actual events is purely coincidental.

PRINTED IN THE U.S.A.

# one

*May 1, 1869*
*Prescott, Arizona Territory*

"Two bowls of venison stew, one order of roast beef, and one of fried chicken. And some of whatever the couple at the next table are having for dessert."

"That's dried peach cobbler." Jenny Davis smiled at the man seated with his young family at the front table of the Capital Restaurant & Bakery.

"Mmm. Can I just skip the stew and start with that, Pa?" the older of two freckle-faced boys asked.

Jenny laughed along with the boy's parents. Heading back to the kitchen, she repeated their order to Elizabeth O'Roarke, the restaurant's owner and Jenny's dearest friend.

"I'm going to set aside four pieces of this cobbler," she told Elizabeth. "That little boy's eyes lit up like he hadn't had a sweet in months!" She didn't mention the pleasure she felt at knowing one of her own baked creations had produced such a craving.

Elizabeth grinned at Jenny, her hazel eyes glowing with pride. "If he thinks it looks good, just wait until he tries a bite. You've developed a real knack for improving the recipes we started out with."

Jenny basked in Elizabeth's praise while she served the family their supper and tended to the other patrons in the crowded dining room. In the two years she'd worked at the restaurant, Elizabeth had taught her a great deal—not only the finer points of turning out mouthwatering pies, cakes, and pastries, but the meaning of friendship and loyalty as well.

She owed a lot to Elizabeth and her husband, Michael. Far more than she would ever be able to repay by waiting tables and helping in the kitchen. Being rescued carried a high price.

And the O'Roarkes had come to her rescue more than once. First from the local saloon keeper her unscrupulous guardian had traded her to for a supply of whiskey. Then again after her former guardian and the saloon keeper kidnapped her in an effort to regain their lost "property."

It had taken many months for Jenny to make the transformation from the frightened girl Elizabeth and Michael had taken under their wing to the more confident young woman she had become. During those months, she had learned what it was like to belong again, to feel like part of a family—a person of worth. Despite her initial sullenness and mistrust, both the O'Roarkes believed in her. And that belief had made all the difference.

She smiled at Elizabeth when she pushed through the swinging door to the kitchen. "If it wasn't almost closing time, you could probably keep on serving for hours yet. Business is going well."

Elizabeth beamed. "Isn't it wonderful how God has continued to bless us?"

They believed in God, too, something Jenny didn't begrudge them in the least. She just wished they wouldn't try to keep pushing their perception of Jenny's need for Him down her throat. Faith was a wonderful thing, as long as the object of your faith lived up to His obligation to take care of His people. When He allowed awful things to happen to them, as He'd done with Jenny and her family, it was hard to muster up the unquestioning trust that seemed to come so easily to Elizabeth and Michael.

That topic had been the only real point of disagreement Jenny and Elizabeth ever had, a point on which Jenny adamantly dug in her heels and refused to budge.

"But everyone has faith in something," Elizabeth had argued

more than once. "What do you have faith in?"

That was easy: herself. She didn't tell Elizabeth that, though. She knew all too well the look of sadness that would fill her friend's eyes. Instead, she always shrugged and said she was still trying to figure that out.

The truth was, she had settled the issue in her mind a long time ago—back when she cowered in a root cellar, listening to the screams of her dying parents and little brother at the hands of Apache warriors.

Back when Martin Lester, her guardian, decided he wanted to treat her more as a wife than a foster daughter. . . back when he tired of her fending him off and traded her to Burleigh Ames, the owner of the Nugget Saloon. . .back when she knew beyond a doubt that if God had loved Jenny Davis once, He didn't any longer. How could a God of love allow all the things that had happened to her?

She wet a rag and carried it to the dining room, where she proceeded to wipe down the empty tables. The family at the front finished their meal and got ready to take their leave.

"That was sure good cobbler," called the little boy. "I hope Pa brings us in again soon."

Jenny smiled at the departing family. The door opened again just after they left, and Michael O'Roarke strolled in.

"Is Elizabeth ready to go? We can enjoy a twilight stroll and still get to the Bible study on time for once if we leave now."

Jenny laughed and nodded toward the rear of the room. "She's in the kitchen. She should just about be finished now. If she isn't, I'll take care of anything that's left so you can be on your way."

Michael grinned at her offer. "Thanks. I appreciate it. You're sure you don't want to go with us?"

"Not this time." It had been her standard answer for the past two years. She was thankful that neither one of them seemed to take offense.

Elizabeth hurried in from the kitchen, wiping her hands

on a towel. "I think I have everything put to rights back there. The dough is rising for tomorrow morning." She patted her hair into place and turned to Jenny. "You're sure—"

"I already asked her," Michael put in with a smile. "Not this time."

Elizabeth nodded, and Michael pulled down the shades covering the front windows while the two women began to blow out the lamps.

"We'll probably head straight home after the Bible study," Elizabeth told Jenny. "Make sure the front door is locked securely after we leave."

"I will." Jenny waited until the two of them set off down Cortez Street, then dropped the bar across the front door. She hadn't needed the reminder. Even when she and Elizabeth both made their home in the rear of the restaurant, securing the place for the night had always been a high priority. Now that she lived there alone, she took even more precautions.

After blowing out the last lamp in the dusky dining room, she pushed through the swinging door into the kitchen, lit the lamp on the counter, then made her way through the kitchen to her room, which had once been Elizabeth's. She set the lamp on the dresser, dropped onto her bed, and reached for her hairbrush. Pulling the brush slowly through her long curls, she thought about her friends and what a nice couple they made. Maybe God really did have a hand in bringing the two of them together. Wouldn't it be nice if He would bring someone as wonderful as Michael into her own life? But she knew she couldn't count on His intervention for that. . .or anything else.

No, she couldn't expect any help from the Almighty. He'd proven that more than once. Michael and Elizabeth would argue the point, of course, but they'd never faced the things Jenny had. Never seen their whole world ripped asunder so that they despaired of ever piecing the fragments back together again.

And they had never been forced to work in a place like the Nugget, singing to the customers, praying her voice would draw in enough extra business to satisfy Burleigh Ames so he wouldn't make good on his threats to force her to do more.

Two years later, the memory of the short time she'd spent in the saloon made Jenny shudder. Shame, raw fear, and her naïveté about the rights of her new guardian had kept her from running away. But unlike the other girls in Burleigh's employ, she had never taken one of the customers upstairs to her room. Even so, having to endure the leers, the comments, and the pawing hands of the customers downstairs left her feeling soiled.

No, God couldn't love her anymore. Not after that. His people were pure, like Elizabeth and Michael. People who went to church and to Bible studies, who prayed expecting answers, and got them. She'd given up on God's love. She knew she wasn't worthy of it. The past had tainted her beyond redemption, and she accepted that fact. All she wanted to do now was forget.

If only other people would let her.

Jenny changed into her nightgown, then slipped barefoot through the darkened kitchen and dining room to check the locks on the doors one last time. Moonlight filtered through a crack in the shades, giving her enough light to accomplish her purpose. She gripped the bar and shook it. Yes, it rested solidly in place.

Jenny turned to go, and her foot struck something, sending the object skittering across the floor like a dry leaf. With a sense of dread, she located it in the dim light and bent to pick it up. She held the thin, folded sheet of paper between her fingers, knowing before she ever opened it what she would find.

*No, please. Not again.*

❧

Andrew Garrett gazed across the broad valley below him. On

the other side of that valley, the ground rose up again, the last in the series of low hills he had crossed that day. Beyond that, according to the directions he'd been given, would be the town of Prescott. *A nice place to build a town,* he reflected. Plenty of piñon, pines, and juniper trees and rolling slopes dotted with manzanita. Nothing like Denver, but a pretty spot all the same.

He urged his horse forward and continued across the valley's level floor, crossing a creek before he came to the last hill. When he reached the top, he pulled his horse to a halt and surveyed the scene before him.

Prescott. A town on the rise, to all appearances. In the neighborhood of a couple of thousand inhabitants, he'd guess. That wouldn't include the others outside the town proper who toiled away at their sluice boxes or knelt in the cold streams, endlessly swirling their gold pans in the hope of finding a nugget.

The gold rush that hit Prescott five years before hadn't been as big as the rush to California in '49. Still, a considerable amount of ore had already been shipped to San Francisco. The question was, how much was still left for the taking?

Which was the question that brought Andrew to Arizona Territory. Flush with the proceeds from their investments in local mines, the Denver Consolidated Mining Company had decided to investigate other likely regions and hired Andrew to use his expertise as a mining engineer to scout out the prospects in Arizona. If the underground ore proved to be as rich as rumor had it, he had been authorized to purchase claims in the name of the group of investors.

Andrew studied the bustling town below him, lying in a basin edged by large pine trees. Mountains rose in the distance to the south, and a large, thumb-shaped butte dominated the landscape in the west. Most of the activity seemed to be centered on the area surrounding a broad, open square that reminded him of Santa Fe's town plaza.

Nothing like Denver's more polished atmosphere, but the same brash spirit, the same feeling of heady optimism he'd experienced in other locales in the midst of a mining boom. The same certainty that the next big strike was just about to happen. But hope alone wouldn't carry the day. Sound investments required a solid foundation, and that was just what Andrew's training had equipped him to look for.

Andrew touched his heels to his horse's flanks and set off down the hill. The men who flocked to the gold fields were the same everywhere, sure the next big strike would be on the claim they owned. Andrew's job was to see if he could make that dream a certainty for the Denver investors.

❧

"Are you going to tell me what's wrong?"

Jenny spun around at the sound of Elizabeth's voice. Managing a shaky laugh at her nervous reaction, she attempted a casual smile. "These raisin tarts. I can't seem to get the dough right."

Elizabeth stepped across the kitchen and squeezed a pinch of the dough between her fingers. "It's a little dry, don't you think? Try adding just a bit more water."

She turned back to Jenny, holding her with a steady gaze that made Jenny wish she could disappear. "What's going on? You don't make mistakes like that."

"Except for when I forgot the baking powder and the biscuits were like rocks. And don't forget the time I put the salt in those piecrusts twice. Remember how that poor man's eyes watered when he bit into it?"

"Months ago, on both counts. Don't try to distract me. This has nothing to do with pastry making. Own up, now. What's wrong?"

Jenny opened her mouth to make a light comment but thought better of it. Trying to sidetrack Elizabeth once she had her mind set on something was like trying to persuade a terrier to part with a cherished bone. She wiped the crumbly dough from her hands with a tea towel and fished a piece of paper from her apron pocket. She handed it over without a word and turned back to add drops of water to her dough.

Behind her, Elizabeth gasped. "Where did this come from?"

"Someone slipped it under the front door last night. I found it after you left."

"I can't believe anyone would write these things." Elizabeth shook the paper under Jenny's nose.

Jenny turned away again. She didn't need to be reminded. The words were forever etched in her memory. *Harlot. Fallen woman. Go back to Whiskey Row.*

Elizabeth studied the wrinkled paper and glanced up at Jenny. "You crumpled this up, then smoothed it out and kept it. Why?"

Jenny shrugged. How could she explain an action she didn't understand herself? Her first thought had been to wad the ugly note into a ball, light a match, and send it into oblivion. Instead, she'd picked the wrinkled folds apart, spread the hateful message open, and folded it neatly in her pocket. Why, indeed? She looked up to find Elizabeth still watching her.

"Do you have any idea who did this?" Elizabeth's voice was sharp.

"No." Jenny gave a short laugh. "And believe me, I spent most of the night trying to figure that out."

Elizabeth's brow furrowed, and she grasped Jenny's arm. "You don't suppose Martin Lester is still around?"

"I don't think so." Even the mention of her erstwhile guardian brought a tightening in her chest. "Last I heard, he'd pulled out and left the territory. He can stay gone forever, for all I care."

"Then who?" Elizabeth waved the note. "This didn't get here all by itself." When Jenny didn't reply, she lifted a burner from the cookstove and dropped the note into the glowing coals. "There. It's gone."

Jenny watched the paper blacken at the edges, then fold in

upon itself before it burst into flames and turned to ash. All well and good, and perhaps it would let Elizabeth think she'd put the hateful words to rest.

As for her, it would take more than mere flames to erase the message from her heart.

❧

Jenny carried a tray laden with flapjacks and bacon to a table near the front window. After an unexpectedly large breakfast rush, the steady stream of customers had dwindled to a trickle, letting Elizabeth leave the kitchen long enough to help clear the empty tables. Maybe the two of them could catch their breath if the lunch crowd held off for a bit.

Jenny removed the last plate of flapjacks from her tray and set it on the table. "That ought to satisfy even a hungry man's appetite." She smiled at the four robust miners, then scanned the room. Two women had just seated themselves at a corner table. She wove her way across the room to greet them.

"Good morning, ladies. Are you ready to order?"

The woman sitting nearest her looked up with a pleasant smile. "I believe I'll have the eggs and biscuits," she began.

The woman on the other side of her tapped the speaker on the shoulder. She leaned over and whispered to her companion, shielding their faces with her spread fingers.

The first woman stared up at Jenny. "That's the one? Oh!" Her smile faded and her gaze darted around the room. "Excuse me," she called to Elizabeth, who was hurrying past with a load of dirty dishes. "Could you take our order, please?"

Elizabeth halted beside Jenny with a puzzled frown. "Didn't you. . ." Her voice trailed off as comprehension spread across her face. Her mouth set in a grim line.

"It's all right," Jenny told her through stiff lips. "I'll take these things back to the kitchen." She lifted the dishes out of Elizabeth's arms and strode into the kitchen.

Setting the dishes on the counter with a clatter, she knotted her hands into fists and pressed them against her flaming cheeks. Would it never end?

Probably not. News spread all too quickly in a close-knit community like Prescott. News and gossip both—hateful, hurtful words, spreading like a deadly plague from one person to the next.

Her stomach roiled and she clapped one hand over her mouth until the acid taste went away. At least Elizabeth hadn't ordered the women out of the restaurant, as she'd been known to do to customers who had impugned Jenny's reputation in the past. While Jenny appreciated her friend's loyalty, the uproar involved and the stares and whispers from the remaining customers were as hard to bear as the insults themselves.

The swinging door burst open, admitting Elizabeth, her eyes blazing with anger. Her expression softened when she saw Jenny's distress.

"I'm sorry," she said, hurrying to wrap her arm around Jenny's shoulders. "So sorry."

The show of sympathy proved to be Jenny's undoing. "Look at me," she whispered through her tears, not wanting her words to carry to the patrons in the dining room. "What do you see? Is there something about me that screams, 'This woman once worked in a saloon, avoid her, lest you be tainted, too'?"

"Of course not. It isn't—"

"Then why does it keep on happening? You know working in the Nugget wasn't something I chose to do. I never would have entered the doors of that place if I hadn't been taken there by force. Doesn't that count for something?" She slapped her hand against the counter. "I've done everything I can think of to show people I'm a decent person. All I want to do is leave the past behind me. Why won't they let me do that?"

"I don't know," Elizabeth said, wiping away her own tears. "I truly don't. But no matter how horrible other people may be, always remember I'm your friend." She pulled Jenny close. "And I'll be praying for you."

*Don't bother.* Jenny nodded her thanks and moved back to

the counter to chop vegetables to put in the stew that would be on the evening's menu. Not for the world would she intentionally hurt Elizabeth's feelings, but her friend might as well save her breath. Jenny knew all too well the futility of calling out to a God who didn't care about her.

If anything were going to turn her life around, she would have to be the one to make it happen.

# two

Andrew Garrett strolled across the plaza, enjoying the scent of pines and the odor of fresh-cut lumber emanating from the sawmill. He scanned the signs on the various businesses facing the open square until he found the one he sought: the Capital Restaurant & Bakery. A simple enough edifice, but surface looks, as he had discovered long ago in his line of work, didn't necessarily reflect what lay within. Earl Waggoner had told him the place served the best food in town.

The corner of his mouth quirked up into a half smile. Apparently, the owner hadn't seen fit to change the name, even though Prescott had lost its status of territorial capital to Tucson two years previously. Maybe they saw it as a statement of the quality of the food. He grinned at the thought.

Inside the modest dining room, he looked around for Waggoner but didn't spot him. No matter. When he and Lute Bledsoe discussed the purchase of Bledsoe's mining claim the day before, Waggoner had stepped up and introduced himself as the miner's agent. Waggoner's slick attitude had struck Andrew wrong at the time, but knowing Bledsoe couldn't read the contract he was offering, he could understand the miner's need for someone to look after his interests. He had to admit, though, that a few moments to enjoy his meal before he had to share table space with Waggoner would help him keep his appetite.

A petite, dark-haired woman stopped to take his order of roast beef and new potatoes, then left Andrew free to study the faces of the other patrons, a pastime he thoroughly enjoyed. The table he'd chosen near the kitchen gave him a good view of the whole room.

If he didn't miss his guess, the young family near the front window had come into town from their farm for supplies. Their simple, threadbare clothing spoke of people who had to pinch their pennies. Enjoying a meal she hadn't cooked herself was probably a rare luxury for the thin-faced wife. Her husband beamed throughout the meal, obviously proud of being able to provide her with this treat.

What about the lone diner in the far corner? Andrew summed up the man's slicked-back, dark hair and flashy clothing in one word: gambler. He'd seen plenty of those around Denver. This fellow would fit right in with them.

He smiled his thanks when the waitress set his order before him. *Mmm.* If the fragrant aroma gave any indication of the taste, Waggoner hadn't exaggerated his claims about the quality of the restaurant's food a bit. Andrew lifted a bite of the roast to his lips and closed his eyes, the better to savor the home-cooked flavor.

Just the way roast beef ought to taste. Not at all the bland fare he might have expected from a small-town restaurant. He'd eaten in the finest dining establishments from St. Louis to San Francisco. This food would hold its own with any of them.

A bright shaft of light beamed across the floor when the front door opened. Earl Waggoner paused in the doorway until he caught sight of Andrew, then hurried over to join him.

"Sorry to be late." Waggoner took off his hat and set it on the corner of the empty chair next to him. "I was unavoidably detained."

"Don't mention it," Andrew said. "As you can see, I've already started eating. Why don't you order, and we can talk business after we've finished?"

"No need to wait on my account. I'd just as soon get down to business right now." Waggoner flagged down the waitress and ordered beef stew and biscuits, then pulled out a folded paper and pushed it across the table to Andrew.

"Here is my authorization to act as agent for Lute Bledsoe.

As he told you yesterday, he can't even sign his own name, let alone read a sales contract. That's why he's asked me to take care of all this on his behalf. You've already made the verbal agreement with him." He paused as the waitress set down his food, then continued, "I'm just here to finalize the legal end of things."

Andrew chewed another bite of beef and took his time studying the paper. He couldn't put his finger on just what it was about Waggoner that gave him pause, but something about the man set off warning bells in Andrew's brain. "Where is Bledsoe?" he asked casually.

Waggoner chuckled. "He left early this morning. Said he was going out to find another claim that would bring in even more money than this one."

Andrew set down the sheet and gave it a last looking over before handing it back to Waggoner. "Everything appears to be in order." *Unfortunately.*

"Good." Waggoner wolfed down his last bite of stew and rubbed his napkin across his mouth, then carefully wiped each end of his mustache. "Let's get down to it, then."

He wadded his napkin and dropped it onto his plate. Shoving the plate aside, he planted his elbows on the table and leaned toward Andrew. "My understanding is that you offered to purchase Bledsoe's claim for the sum of five hundred dollars. Is that correct?"

"That's what we agreed on." Andrew pulled a sheaf of papers from his coat pocket and handed them to Waggoner. "You can read the contract for yourself. It's a fair price."

"Bledsoe is more than satisfied with that amount. And I'm sure your Colorado group would feel they've made a good bargain." Waggoner's thin lips spread and lifted his mustache in a wolfish grin. "But what about you?"

"Me?" The question startled Andrew. "I'm hired to acquire properties at the best price possible. My own concern in this is to be sure the agreement is fair to both parties.

I believe I've done that."

"But are you getting enough out of the deal?"

"I told you, I'm in the employ of the Denver Consolidated Mining Company. I don't have a financial interest in the deal."

"Then you're missing out on some easy money." Waggoner's eyes held an eager light. "I have a proposition for you. Write out a new agreement, but make the selling price on this one seven hundred dollars. That's still low enough that it won't raise any concern from your investors."

The faint warning bells grew into clanging gongs. Andrew tried to keep his voice calm. "Are you telling me Bledsoe has changed his mind and wants to raise his price?"

Waggoner snorted. "Bledsoe won't know anything about it. He'll get the money he's expecting and that will be all, as far as he's concerned."

"Then the additional money. . ." Andrew let his voice trail off, waiting for Waggoner to finish the thought.

"Will be split between you and me, fifty-fifty." Waggoner leaned back and laced his fingers across his stomach. "A nice little profit for both of us, don't you agree?"

"No. I don't agree." Andrew shoved his chair back and stood, towering over the other man. "Have you ever done any mining? Ever squatted for hours in an icy stream on a placer claim, scooping up pan after pan of gravel and swirling it back and forth, waiting to spot just one bit of gold dust? Ever spent days on end shaking a rocker until you thought your arms were ready to fall off?"

He planted his fists on the table and leaned over, just inches from Waggoner's face. "Well, I have, and I'm here to tell you it's brutally hard work. Bledsoe located that claim through his own sweat and determination. He didn't try to make a killing on this deal. He just wanted a fair price in return for his labor. I don't hold with covert transactions. If you can't let your business dealings be known in public, there's something wrong with them."

He tucked the contract back inside his inner coat pocket. "I'll hand Bledsoe his money directly. And I'll make sure he knows exactly how you planned to repay his trust."

"If you can find him." Waggoner sneered. "He's out in the Bradshaws by now."

"No, he isn't." A gray-haired man at a neighboring table turned toward them. "I saw him just this morning, over at Bowen Mercantile. Said he was waiting for some money so he could stock up on supplies before he headed out." He fixed Waggoner with a level gaze. "This young fellow won't be the only one spreading the word about how you do business. No one will trust you to so much as hold his horse for him by the time this day is out."

Waggoner's expression now reminded Andrew more of a slinking coyote than a hungry wolf. "I'll get to Bledsoe first and block the sale. No one's going to make a profit out of this." He stormed out, leaving a relieved silence behind him.

❧

Jenny drew away from the swinging door and turned her attention back to dishing up the next order. Altercations like that weren't commonplace in the restaurant, unless you counted Elizabeth springing to Jenny's defense whenever some unwise customer made a disparaging remark about her background. The raised voices had caught her notice; the words that carried through the door riveted her attention.

She hadn't recognized either of the voices, although she felt an immediate distrust for Waggoner, just by hearing his oily tone.

The other man, though—that rich baritone inspired confidence, even without a glimpse of his face.

Jenny sliced another serving of roast and set it on a plate, her curiosity piqued by the argument she had heard. Most of their customers wouldn't be so scrupulous about turning down an easy profit.

Good thing this one had. Jenny knew Bledsoe as one of

the miners who frequented the restaurant. Knew him and liked him. He'd worked hard to find that claim. He didn't deserve to be cheated by some unscrupulous would-be agent.

Apparently, the mellow-voiced man felt the same way. Jenny's mind raced while she ladled out a helping of carrots. What manner of man would behave that way? And for someone he didn't even know?

His actions didn't mesh with what she'd seen in the majority of the men she'd known. After her experiences with Martin Lester, Burleigh Ames, and the customers at the Nugget, Jenny had pretty much given up on men altogether. If she were ever going to be interested in a man, he would have to be one with the mellow-voiced stranger's brand of integrity.

"Jenny?" Elizabeth came through the swinging door, her face alight with curiosity. "There's a customer out there who wants to talk to you."

"With me?" Jenny threw a wary glance toward the dining room. "Who is it?"

Elizabeth shook her head. "I've never seen him before. And he didn't mention you by name, just asked if he could speak with the cook."

Jenny smoothed her apron and patted her hair into place, pondering the strange request. A sudden thought struck her. Could it be the man she'd just heard? The one who put another man's welfare ahead of his own gain? Her heart quickened at the idea of meeting him face-to-face.

Hoping her face wasn't too flushed from the heat of the kitchen, she pushed open the door and stepped into the dining room.

# three

After Waggoner stomped out, Andrew realized every gaze in the restaurant was turned his way. Let them look. He knew he'd raised his voice and lost his temper, but he didn't see how he could have done otherwise. The idea of Waggoner fleecing both Bledsoe and the group of investors galled him. The agent's casual assumption that Andrew would be willing to go along with the plan sickened him.

The dark-haired man Andrew had taken for a gambler raised his hand and called the waitress over. She spoke to him, then hurried off to the kitchen, and the customers turned back to their meals.

Andrew fished in his pocket. He'd pay his bill and get out of there while he was no longer the center of attention. It looked like he'd be paying Waggoner's bill, too, he noted grimly. One more black mark against the man's name.

The kitchen door swung open again, and a slender young woman stepped into the dining room. Andrew's breath caught in his throat. Her face could have come straight out of a Gainsborough portrait. Curly blond bangs hung loosely over her high forehead. The rest of her hair, pulled up to the crown of her head in the back, descended in ringlets to just below her shoulders.

She glanced around the room, her blond curls reflecting glints of copper in the light that streamed in through the front window. Then her blue-green gaze met Andrew's, and for a moment his heart felt like it had frozen in his chest.

Who was she? What was she like? Everything within him yearned to find the answers to those questions.

But that would take time. Time he didn't have. The Denver

Consolidated Mining Company trusted him to carry out the job they'd hired him to do. As soon as he paid Bledsoe, he had to head down to Tucson to investigate the rumors of gold, silver, and copper in the southern part of the territory.

Once he'd finished his business there, though, he might just come back and make the acquaintance of the girl with the coppery highlights in her hair. It would give him a reason to complete his business in Tucson as quickly as possible.

For now, though. . . He tore his gaze away, left his money on the table, and stepped through the door to find the Bowen Mercantile and talk to Lute Bledsoe.

☙

Jenny caught sight of a tall, sandy-haired man staring at her. Her heart sped up even more. Could this be the one who had asked to speak with her? Then he looked away, set some money on the table, and walked out.

With a sense of loss, she watched him go, then scanned the rest of the room. A man in the far corner beckoned to her. He rose to greet her as she made her way to his table.

"Are you the one responsible for the delicious meal I've just enjoyed?" He favored her with a slight bow. "Allow me to introduce myself. My name is Evan Townsend."

Jenny took in his frock coat and embroidered vest. Coupled with his confident air, they reminded her of some of the habitués of the Nugget's gaming tables. "How do you do? I'm Jenny Davis." She offered her hand, wondering why he had summoned her.

His soft fingers enveloped hers in a warm grip. "And you truly are the one who did the cooking today? The ham, the crumb cake?"

Jenny nodded. "Elizabeth and I share the cooking duties, but I did fix those."

His eyes glowed. "Beauty and talent in the same package. A rare find."

Jenny withdrew her hand and clasped her fingers behind

her. "I need to get back to the kitchen, Mr. Townsend. If that's all you wanted. . . ?"

"No, wait. Forgive me for not coming straight to the point. I'd like to discuss a business proposition with you. Sit down." He pulled out a chair and flashed a brilliant smile. "Please."

Every instinct told Jenny to turn on her heel and march back to the kitchen. She'd had enough experience with bold men and their business schemes to last a lifetime. She studied Evan Townsend and his assured smile. At least he'd asked her to stay, not ordered her to. Still, everything about him spoke of a man used to getting his own way. If she had any sense, she ought to get out of his reach before he spoke another word.

To her amazement, she sat.

Evan's smile lit up the dim corner where they sat. "Thank you." He pushed in her chair and seated himself directly across from her. "Miss Davis, I'm a businessman. I have various holdings throughout the territory: part ownership in a freighting company in La Paz; a lumber mill not far from here; a store near Camp Verde. Right now, I'm focusing on starting some new ventures in Tucson."

Jenny nodded distractedly, her mind back on the tasks going undone in the kitchen. With Elizabeth back there at the moment, she knew nothing would be left to scorch on the stove. But there were still carrots to slice and potatoes to put on to boil. And that last batch of rolls should be finished rising.

Evan Townsend went on. "I'll admit Tucson hasn't been much of a showplace, but things have been changing since the territorial capital moved there two years ago. There are opportunities for a man who knows how to make things happen." He settled back in his chair and looked straight at her. "A man like me, Miss Davis."

"That's very interesting, Mr. Townsend. Now I really must—"

"I've purchased a building in a favorable location. Granted, it's small, but space can be added as needed. It's an ideal spot, close to the center of the action. There's plenty of profit to be made, and I'm just the man to do it."

Those rolls would be ready to overflow their pan if she didn't get back to them. Jenny pushed back her chair and stood, eager to escape this flow of information. "It was nice meeting you, Mr. Townsend."

He scrambled to his feet, a crestfallen expression twisting his features. "Then you're not interested?"

"Interested?" His astonishment made it apparent she'd missed something. But what?

"I thought I'd made it clear. I intend to open a restaurant in Tucson. I'll provide the building and the start-up capital, but I need someone with excellent cooking skills to make it a profitable investment. As soon as I tasted that meal, I knew I'd found one cook in a million." His face lightened again as he looked at her. "And once I met you, that sealed my decision. What do you say? Will you come in with me as my partner? Your culinary skills and my business acumen. We'll split the profits right down the middle."

Jenny's mind reeled. That was the second business proposal she'd heard in less than an hour. Both promised substantial earnings. Only one of them sounded honorable. And that one had been directed at her.

But leave Prescott? Part company with Elizabeth and Michael? She shook her head. "No, thank you, Mr. Townsend. Your opinion of my cooking is flattering, but my home is here. I couldn't think of leaving."

Disappointment shadowed his handsome features, then he gave a quick shrug. "You win some, you lose some." He reached into his vest pocket and dropped several coins on the table. "I'll be in town for two more days. I'm staying at the Prescott House. Let me know if you change your mind."

Jenny watched him stride away, then retreated to the safe familiarity of the kitchen. It would take more—much more—than a stranger's pretty promises to make her decide to uproot and leave.

❧

"Talk some sense into her, Michael. I've tried everything." Elizabeth leaned against a cupboard and folded her arms across her chest as though distancing herself from the conversation.

Her husband gave Jenny an apologetic smile. "We only want what's best for you." He spread his hands wide. "You must know how much we both care about you."

Jenny's throat tightened. Of course she knew they cared. Without Elizabeth and Michael putting their very lives on the line to come to her rescue, she'd be living a life of degradation in the Nugget now.

"I can never repay what you've done for me," she began. "Without your help, I know only too well the kind of life I would have been forced into. Being freed of that was the best thing that ever happened to me." Her throat tightened. "But I'm not completely free, even now."

Michael's brow wrinkled in consternation. In answer to his unspoken question, Jenny reached into her pocket and held up a folded slip of paper. "Some people haven't forgotten where I've been, and they won't let me forget, either." She pressed the paper into Michael's hand and watched his eyebrows soar halfway to his hairline as he read.

"That's abominable!" He crumpled the sheet and tossed it from him. "But you can't let one incident push you into a hasty decision."

"It isn't just this once," Elizabeth interjected reluctantly. "This is the second one she's gotten."

"The fifth," Jenny corrected.

Elizabeth whirled and stared at her. "There've been more? All slipped under the door like these two? Why didn't you tell me?"

Jenny shrugged and picked at a loose thread on her cuff. "I tried to ignore them. I don't know, maybe I thought if I didn't mention them, they'd quit coming. It didn't work, though, did it?" The laugh she attempted caught in her throat.

"You mean to tell me someone's been sneaking around here at night and shoving these under the door?" Michael's voice rose to a near bellow.

"Not all of them. I found others out at the woodpile and stuck to the top of the barrel where I take out the trash. Whoever is doing this wants to make sure their messages reach me."

"But Michael's right," Elizabeth put in. "You can't make choices based on the action of one hateful individual."

"You don't understand." Jenny stared at her two dearest friends. How could they possibly comprehend the pain of being reminded about her unsavory past? "It isn't just whoever is writing these notes. Think about it, Elizabeth. How many times over the past two years have you gone to my defense when some customer mentioned my time at the Nugget?"

Elizabeth focused on a spot on the floor and didn't answer.

"It doesn't matter how hard I try to shake off the memories. There are people here who will never stop bringing it up." Jenny looked around the kitchen that had become so familiar, her heart aching at the thought of leaving it behind. "I thought I could keep ignoring these, but I can't. Even if we found out who's been leaving the notes and made them stop, it wouldn't change what's in people's minds. To some, I'll always be nothing more than a saloon girl. The only way I can get away from that is to leave."

Elizabeth's eyes glistened with unshed tears. She moved next to Michael, as if drawing comfort from his nearness. "Then there's nothing we can do to change your mind?"

Jenny blinked back tears of her own and gazed at her friends intently, imprinting their images on her memory so she could carry them with her in her heart. "It's something I have to do. I'll go over to the Prescott House first thing in the morning and tell Evan Townsend I've decided to take him up on his offer."

# four

*Hot.*

Jenny stood in the minute bit of shade provided by the doorway of the adobe building Evan had named the Pueblo Restaurant. Heat rose in shimmering waves along the dusty street.

She pulled a handkerchief from her sleeve and used it to mop the perspiration from her face and neck. Her fingers twiddled with her top button. Did she dare loosen it? Modesty said no; comfort said yes. Comfort won out.

*Ahh.* Even that slight difference gave some relief. Jenny raised her hand to shield her eyes from the blazing afternoon sun. When she first arrived in Tucson, she found it hard to believe this could be the same sun that had illuminated the Prescott sky. Back home, it was a welcome friend, urging the chilly spring mornings toward the promise of summer warmth. This sun was relentless in its oppressive heat, searing the desert landscape.

The fiery orb hovered a little past its zenith. In Prescott, the day's activity would continue unabated. Here, the streets lay deserted, the population having retired indoors for their afternoon siesta. Later, when the scorching temperatures lessened, the town would come back to life.

Jenny picked up a damp rag and waved it back and forth, fanning a cooling breeze across her face. It was a harsh land, an arid land. And yet, unlikely as it seemed, it had become *her* land.

Looking along the Calle del Arroyo, she could see the

Tucson Mountains in the distance, their barren peaks devoid of the forest that covered the slopes in the northern part of the territory. A desolate wasteland at first glance, until one looked beyond the bleak landscape and saw beauty in the spreading arms of the saguaro, the scarlet blooms atop the spindly ocotillo branches. The wide vistas invited her to lose herself in their vast expanse, and Jenny welcomed the opportunity. Here, an anonymous speck in a broad universe, she finally felt free of her past.

She had come here looking for sanctuary, a place where she could start anew. She had found all that and more.

*And now I'd better find a place to get out of the sun.* Jenny laughed softly. The custom of resting during the hottest part of the day had seemed peculiar at first. After only a few days of pushing herself to keep working throughout the afternoon hours, she had embraced the local wisdom without question.

"You're still here?"

Jenny turned at the sound of a voice behind her. Evan leaned against the adobe wall, a friendly smile playing across his face. *About time he showed up.* Jenny hadn't seen him around the restaurant at all that day. He must have slipped in through the office door.

"I was just getting ready to leave." Jenny stepped past him to retrieve her bonnet from its peg on the wall of the small corner office.

"May I accompany you? There are a couple of things I'd like to discuss."

Jenny locked the front door and tucked her hand into the crook of Evan's arm. They strolled along the deserted street at an easy pace, their feet sending up tiny puffs of dust with every step.

She ducked her head against the bright glare that even the bonnet's wide brim couldn't block. Perhaps she should carry a parasol. At this rate, her fair skin would soon be a mass of blisters and freckles. And that might not be a bad thing. Her looks had caused her nothing but trouble and heartache thus far.

Evan broke into her thoughts. "I'm concerned about you. You've been working too hard. I wanted a business partner for this venture, not a slave."

Jenny chuckled and gave his arm a reassuring pat. "It's freedom I've found here, Evan, not slavery. For the first time, I'm building up something substantial for my future, something I can be proud of. You have no idea what that means to me."

Evan halted abruptly. Placing his fingers beneath her chin, he tilted her head up to face him. "Still, I'm worried about you. When I asked you to come here, I hadn't counted on problems arising with my other business interests. I didn't plan on being called away almost as soon as the restaurant got underway, and I never expected you to take on the business responsibilities in addition to doing all the cooking. You're spending far more time here than I ever intended."

"But don't you see, Evan? I've found out I'm able to do more than just cook. The menu planning, ordering supplies, keeping the books—having the responsibility for all those details is new to me, but I'm good at it." She gave him a brilliant smile. "I feel like I've finally found my place in life, and I'm loving every minute of it."

"Even in this blast furnace of a place? You aren't inclined to go rushing back to those cool mountain summers at the first opportunity?"

*If you only knew.* Jenny contented herself with a shake of her head. She hadn't told Evan her reasons for leaving Prescott and didn't plan to now. Or ever. That part of her life belonged to the past. This was a place of new beginnings.

"Let's talk about the future," she said. "If what we've brought in so far and our steady increase in customers are anything to go by, we could double our profits by next month."

Evan gave her a look of rueful admiration. "Is there ever a time you aren't thinking about profits?"

She grinned. "Face it, Evan. You've joined forces with a hard-headed businesswoman."

"But a lovely one." His smile grew tender.

Jenny looked away and set off down the street on her own. *Don't spoil it.*

After a moment, she heard Evan's footsteps catching up to her. "I'm not sure what I did to upset you," he said. "But would this hardheaded businesswoman be willing to let me make it up to her by taking her to the playhouse this evening?"

"I don't think so, Evan. There are things I need to do."

"Like what?" Exasperation and amusement mingled in his tone. "Come up with new additions for the menu? You've already done that a dozen times."

"Actually, I was thinking of drawing up plans for a larger dining room. If things keep going as well as they have, we'll need some extra space before long."

For the second time, Evan stopped her, but this time his lips were twitching with suppressed mirth. "Jenny, Jenny. Only a few weeks in Tucson, and already you're planning to expand the business." He threw back his head and laughed. "I didn't hire a cook; I took on the most ambitious business partner in the territory!"

His laughter subsided, but the twinkle in his gray eyes lingered. "Even a tycoon has to take a night off now and then. Think of it as an opportunity to meet new people, potential customers you can lure to the restaurant. Better yet, think of it as a favor to me. I'm ready for a night out, and I need someone to keep an eye on me to make sure I don't spend all our hard-earned money."

Jenny studied his face for a long moment. "All right," she said and resumed walking. "Just this once."

"Wonderful! I'll pick you up at seven." He paused at the door of the house where she rented her small room. "And I'll tell you one thing: As hard a bargain as you drive, I'm glad you're on the same side of our business dealings as I am." He winked and gave her a brief wave as he turned away.

≥a

Jenny peered into her mirror and twisted the last ringlet into place. There. The coppery-blond curl draped over the shoulder of her sapphire-blue princess-cut dress. She smiled, enjoying the novelty of seeing herself dressed for an evening out rather than her usual wilted appearance after a day spent in a hot kitchen or laboring over the restaurant accounts.

Despite the disinterest she'd expressed to Evan, she felt a rising surge of anticipation. She had overheard her customers talk of the playhouses in Tucson, but she had never been to one herself. She'd never expected to, either.

But going out for an evening of entertainment went along with the lifestyle of a respectable woman making her mark in the community. Such a difference from the existence of the past few years, when her foremost goal had been to keep a low profile and hope others would forget her dismal past!

She lifted her new hat from its box. Purchased on impulse along with the blue gown with some of her first earnings from the Pueblo, it had lain untouched until now. With a sense of embarking on an adventure, she set it in place and tilted her head from side to side, studying the effect. Was the froth of ribbons and bows too much?

No, it suited the evening and her buoyant mood. She adjusted it once more, letting the front dip over her forehead.

There. She nodded approvingly at the image in the glass, no longer the solemn-faced girl she usually saw, but the picture of a respectable lady.

A shiver of excitement swept up and down her arms. An evening at the theater, her goal of making herself into the person she longed to be within reach—what other surprises did her new life hold?

Evan knocked at the door of the house promptly at seven. His black frock coat and gleaming white shirt took Jenny's breath away. An attractive man, no doubt about it. And in his evening attire, he looked downright handsome.

From the gleam in his eyes, he approved of her appearance in equal measure, but he forbore to comment. *Good.* Maybe he had learned from her reaction earlier. Whatever the reason, she appreciated his restraint.

The show proved even more wonderful than Jenny had imagined. The glow of the footlights, the cheers from the audience, and the lively music all combined to make it an evening of pure enjoyment.

During the intermission, Jenny strolled to the back of the seating area with Evan. Moving through the crowd, she couldn't miss the admiring glances he drew from the women they passed or the jealous looks they cast at her.

"Having a good time?" Evan bent close, his lips nearly brushing her ear so she could hear him over the noisy throng.

She smiled and nodded, not bothering to try to make herself heard. So this was what it felt like to spend time in the company of a man with no purpose but to enjoy herself, to be the object of envy and not scorn. She could find it easy to get used to this way of life. Very easy, indeed.

Evan placed a cup of punch in Jenny's hands, then led her over to a quiet corner of the room. "May I leave you here for just a moment? I need to discuss a bit of business with some of the gentlemen here." His eyelid dropped in a wink. "Nothing to do with the restaurant, I assure you. I wouldn't dare leave you out of that."

At her nod, he withdrew a few steps to where a small group of men waited.

Jenny sipped the fruity drink and contented herself with watching the milling crowd. One or two of the ladies who glanced her way bowed their heads and smiled a greeting. Jenny returned their nods with pleasure.

Respectability. Acceptance. Everything she had longed for and hadn't been able to achieve in Prescott appeared to be hers for the taking here. Elizabeth would have said a prayer of thanks; Jenny knew she had done it on her own.

Evan returned when the music signaled the end of intermission, trailed by two of his business associates. Just before he reached Jenny, she saw one of them pull him aside and shout to be heard over the crowd.

"I don't blame you for wanting to keep her to yourself," he said with a grin. "My compliments on escorting the most beautiful woman here."

Evan rejoined her and darted a glance over his shoulder at his departing companion. "I hope that didn't bother you," he murmured. "He meant it only as a compliment, I assure you."

"It didn't bother me," Jenny replied, filled with a sense of wonder when she realized it was true. For the first time in years, she didn't mind being admired for her looks. Truly, this place had worked its magic on her.

~

Bright stars glittered across the desert sky. Jenny nestled into her pillow and watched the grand procession through the small window of her room.

*A night like this should last forever.* How long had it been since she'd been around people without bracing herself for the next scathing comment?

The Pleiades edged past the corner of her window. Jenny grinned at the familiar grouping and stretched her arms wide, then laced her fingers behind her head. She might have made some mistakes along the way, but moving to Tucson hadn't been one of them.

Snatches of one of the tunes she heard that night drifted into her mind. She closed her eyes and sang the words softly.

Her eyes snapped open again. She hadn't sung since performing for the crowd of half-drunk customers her last night at the Nugget, just a few hours before Michael O'Roarke rescued her from the dreadful place and spirited her away to safety. Singing always brought back memories of that dark time in her life, and she'd avoided it diligently.

Until now. She whispered a few more of the lyrics and felt something break loose within her. Like a dam weakened by a tiny fissure that grew until it could hold back its wall of water no longer, the protective wall Jenny had built up began to crumble. If it hadn't been the middle of the night, she would have flung off the bed covers and burst forth in full voice.

Tears of joy stung her eyes. Back when her family was laboring to make a living on their Chino Valley farm, singing had been one of the delights of her life. Back then, life meant love, safety, and security. She had thought she'd lost all those forever. Beginning her new life in Tucson had restored her joy in living again.

Her heart swelled in her chest until she thought she'd burst with gladness. After all that had happened, all the years of pain and humiliation, she was finally free.

She hummed a few more bars, reveling in her newfound liberty. Scenes from the evening floated through her memory, the bright lights, the music, the ladies and gentlemen of Tucson dressed in their finest.

Responding to bows and smiles and nods of greeting, and not one of them laced with a sneer of contempt. . . Jenny wanted to soar right out the window and join the stars in their celestial dance.

What was it Evan's friend had called her? The most beautiful woman there? And later, after the evening's entertainment had ended, Evan had introduced her to others of his acquaintance, each of them trying to outdo the flattery of the others.

For once, the praise hadn't bothered her. They had spoken in a friendly manner, with no innuendos or disreputable overtones, and their words acted as a refreshing rain on the parched ground of Jenny's soul.

Would she ever see any of those men again? It would be interesting to see if any of them lived up to their promises to dine at the Pueblo. Would she recognize them if they did?

She had been introduced to such a number of new people, they all seemed to meld into a faceless blur.

Weariness overcame her at last. She rolled onto her side and folded her hands beneath her cheek. One face stood out in her mind, superseding all the others. Who could it be? Her sleepy mind puzzled over the mystery, sorting through the men she'd met that night.

Just before sleep claimed her, the answer came. She hadn't seen him that night at all. The tanned face, sandy hair, and clear blue eyes belonged to the man from Prescott, whose face seemed to be permanently etched in her memory.

❧

"How are you feeling today?" Evan lounged against the kitchen doorway, watching Jenny run a tea towel across a newly washed plate.

"I'm fine," Jenny replied. With the last of the lunch customers gone, she needed only to stack the dishes and wipe down the counters before she closed the doors for the afternoon. "Better than that, actually. I feel absolutely invigorated today."

Evan lifted one eyebrow. "You are aware, aren't you, that it's even hotter today than yesterday?"

"I'm fine," Jenny repeated. "Truly." She scrubbed the last section of the counter and rolled her sleeves back down, buttoning the cuffs in place.

Evan lifted his hands in surrender. "I won't argue with you. I don't have the energy. But I do have an idea how we can relieve you of some of your workload."

"But I don't—"

Evan cleared his throat, cutting off her protest. "You're doing a wonderful job of running the place, and I realize you're enjoying yourself, and that's fine—for now. But I'm looking at it from a larger perspective. What happens if you wear yourself out to the point you get sick? I'd have no trouble taking over the books, but I could never step in and manage the cooking. We'd have to shut the doors, Jenny. Do you want that?"

She stared at him, sobered by the picture his words painted.

He went on. "I want you to consider hiring a helper, someone you can train to cook your way. Think of it as an investment. You can still oversee the kitchen, but with another pair of hands to help, you'll be able to concentrate more on the management end of things. It looks like I'm going to have to spend more time away from here than I thought. I need to be able to count on you to run the whole place, and you can't do it alone."

Jenny squeezed the cleaning rag between her fingers. Evan had a point, especially when it came to giving her more time to do the office work. The discovery that she possessed a keen business mind and enjoyed using it buoyed her spirits. Much as she hated to admit it, though, she did feel tired at the end of the day. So tired, she often had to force herself to stay awake long enough to make the ledger entries and draw up supply orders every evening.

What if she followed Evan's suggestion? She wouldn't want just anyone working in her kitchen. She and Elizabeth had gotten along famously, but that surely wouldn't be the norm.

But the thought of spending more time ensconced in her little office tantalized her. If Evan was right, if she could find someone willing to learn to cook the way she did. . .

"I'll do it." She raised her gaze to his and chuckled at his look of surprise. "I'm a businesswoman, remember? And this will be the best choice for our business. But," she admonished, "you have to promise me one thing."

"What's that?"

Jenny folded her arms and lifted her chin. "Don't go looking for someone to fill the position. This is something I want to do myself."

A slow smile lit Evan's face. "I'm beginning to realize there are a lot of things you want to do for yourself. Have at it, then. You're the lady in charge."

# five

Jenny scooted a shipping crate across the floor of her new dwelling and set it in place next to a straight-backed chair, where it would serve as a small table. She draped a colorful serape over the crate and stood back to observe the effect. What a change this sun-drenched space was from her stuffy little rented room!

She twitched a corner of the serape into place, marveling at the transformation that had taken place in her life. Jenny Davis, businesswoman. Jenny Davis, part owner of the Pueblo Restaurant. And now, Jenny Davis, homeowner.

The concept still seemed foreign to her. Who would have thought the girl whose life had been shattered by tragedy would one day become the proud owner of this small but neat adobe home?

She reached for a jar to use as a vase on her makeshift table, then realized the time. The rest would have to wait until after supper. She yawned and stretched, already feeling the effects of missing her afternoon siesta. In just a few hours, she promised herself, she would be back to finish moving in and enjoy a well-earned night's sleep in her new home.

Outside, the late afternoon sun glinted off the little adobe's whitewashed walls. Jenny paused for a moment to cast a lingering glance at the rosebush blooming beside the front door. It looked like—no, it *was*—a real home. Her home.

Meyer Street had started coming back to life. Jenny passed a donkey-drawn *carreta* and smiled at a group of dust-covered children kicking an empty can along the way. When one of her regular customers called out her name and waved a greeting, she smiled and waved back.

Home. The word meant more than a roof over her head. More, even, than her whitewashed adobe dwelling. It signified a place where she was accepted, a place to belong. For the first time, Jenny felt she'd found that place. A place of contentment, or as near to contentment as a person could expect to come.

Jenny sidestepped a man carrying a load of firewood on his back, then continued her musings. Perfect peace wasn't an attainable goal for people like herself. She knew that and accepted it, even though the knowledge left an aching void she didn't often acknowledge.

Still, life here was good. Better than she had any reason to expect a few short months ago.

Her steps quickened when the Pueblo Restaurant came into view. Here she had a place to call her own and a business where she could indulge in doing the cooking she loved and improve on her newfound business skills. She had no cause for complaint.

She unlocked the front door and gazed around the dining room. In her mind's eye, she could already see the benefits an addition to the building would create. A bigger dining area, first of all. And certainly more kitchen space.

She hung her wide-brimmed bonnet on a peg in her office and hurried to the kitchen to don her apron and prepare the evening meal. Once the pork pie was in the oven, she scrubbed and peeled the potatoes methodically, smiling when she thought of Elizabeth's last letter where her friend had mentioned the possibility of building an addition to the Capital Restaurant & Bakery. Wouldn't she be surprised to hear about Jenny's own plans?

Thoughts of those plans kept her mind occupied while her hands were busy scraping carrots and making biscuits.

The afternoon passed quickly, and, before long, the scrape of the front door followed by the shuffle of feet announced the arrival of the evening's first diner. Jenny did a hasty check to make sure all was in order, then put on a welcoming smile and went to greet her guest.

"Red!" Her smile broadened in genuine pleasure when she recognized her favorite customer. Red Dwyer might not be as dapper and elegant as the men Evan had introduced her to the night before, but his presence never failed to lighten Jenny's spirits.

"And how are you this fine evening, Miss Jenny?" The wiry Irishman removed his floppy felt hat and brushed a light coating of dust off his miner's garb before seating himself at the table he preferred, nearest the kitchen.

"Ready to hear more of your stories about lost mines and buried treasure," Jenny teased. "But first, let me take your order. What would you like tonight?"

"Would you be having any of that pork pie you do so well? All the time I've been out in the Dragoon Mountains, my mouth's been watering for it."

Jenny laughed at the blatant flattery. "And since you're sitting where the aroma floats right out the kitchen door, you know perfectly well that it's on the menu."

Red's eyes glinted with good humor. "Ah, Lass, you've too quick a mind for the likes of me. Bring me a portion of your pork pie, then, and fill the plate to overflowing."

Jenny complied, bringing herself a smaller serving as well. "It looks like a slow night," she said, glancing around at the otherwise empty room. "Mind if I sit with you? You can fill me in on your latest adventures while we eat."

"A succulent meal and the company of a charming lady to go with it?" Red gave a contented sigh. "What more could a man ask for?"

Jenny felt a faint blush rise to her cheeks. Red's constant Irish blarney had made her uncomfortable at first. It had taken her some time before she realized he meant it in a good-natured way and not with the unpleasant familiarity of many of the miners she'd known at the Nugget. Now she treated him with the easy camaraderie of someone she'd known for years rather than a stranger who'd only come into her life a few weeks before.

*It's a little like the way Pa and I used to talk,* she reflected. Red was older than her pa would have been, though. Probably in his mid to late fifties, although his sunbaked face made it hard to judge. And the gray strands that threaded through his dark red hair attested to his advancing years.

But his cheery disposition and sparkling sense of humor showed no signs of age. He took a bite of the pork pie and closed his eyes as if in transports of bliss. "This is it. The very flavor I've been dreaming of these past days." He dug into the rest of his meal with gusto, not speaking again until he had finished and blotted his lips with his napkin. "Jenny, you've saved a desperate man."

Jenny swallowed a bite of her own meal and shook her head. "Enough of the flattery, Red. Let's hear some more of your stories."

"Ah, well. Where shall I begin?" He slurped his coffee and settled back in his chair. "You've heard about me childhood in Clonlara, the fairest spot on the Emerald Isle, correct?"

"Mm-hm. And how you sailed to America to escape the terrible famine in Ireland."

"And my time in Boston up until I decided to follow the lure of riches and headed to the gold-encrusted hills of California to make me fortune?"

Jenny pushed her plate aside and leaned forward, enjoying the banter involved in recounting Red's history. "And instead of finding the mother lode, you barely made enough to keep yourself alive. And so. . ."

"And so I came to search for El Dorado here in Arizona Territory for one last try at making a strike before I get too old to pack up my burro and head off into those tempting hills."

Jenny laughed. Only Red would call the rocky hills surrounding Tucson tempting. She'd heard plenty of other terms for the area: bleak and barren, for starters.

"It must be so different here than where you grew up."

Red ran his hand through his hair and scratched the back of his head. "You're right about that. This heat-blasted country is a far cry from the Emerald Isle, to be sure. On the other hand, there's always that hint of treasure to be found, the promise of fortune lying just ahead. It's drawn me for years. I couldn't turn my back on it now if I wanted to."

Jenny tapped her fingers on the table. "I'm still waiting for my story."

"But, Lass." Red spread his hands wide. "It sounds like you know my life history as well as I do. What more could I be telling?"

"It doesn't matter what you tell; it's the way you tell it. You could spin a grocery list into one of Scheherazade's tales. You've been gone five days. Surely you've had some adventures during that time. Things just don't stay quiet for long when you're around."

"Ah." Red tipped his chair back on two legs and drained the last of his coffee, seeming to ponder Jenny's accolade. "Well, if it's news of my latest wanderings you're wanting, you shall have it."

He rocked his chair forward, setting the front legs back on the clay floor with a thud. He cleared a space in front of him, planted his hands flat on the table, and looked straight into Jenny's eyes. "I've found it, Lass."

"Found what?" she started to ask, but the dancing excitement in his eyes set a certainty growing in her mind.

"Red!" She glanced over her shoulder to make sure the place was still empty, then continued in hushed tones. "You mean you struck it rich out there?"

The wiry man rubbed his palms together and grinned. "The next thing to it, anyway. I've located a vein of silver out there. A big one, by the looks of her. The biggest this old rock pounder has ever seen. I saw a streak of white quartz on the side of a gully and went to check it out. And there she was, just sitting there as if she'd been waiting all these years for me to come along." His eyes gleamed with anticipation. "She's the strike I've dreamed of through all my days of wandering, Lass. I know she is." His pale blue eyes glistened and seemed to focus on a scene far beyond the confines of the restaurant's walls.

Jenny stared in openmouthed wonder, then burst out laughing. "You old scoundrel! How long were you going to keep that to yourself if I hadn't dragged it out of you?"

"I had no fear about that." Red's mouth tweaked up in an impish grin. "Knowing how fond you are of stories, and all."

"So why are you sitting here talking to me instead of heading back out there to bring it out and come back a wealthy man?"

"Ah, there's the problem." Red rubbed his hand along his jawline. "It's a simple enough answer, though. I'm broke." He chuckled at her gasp of dismay. "I have enough to pay for my supper, never fear. And I'm able to pay for my lodging and otherwise keep body and soul together for the time being. But enough to finance the equipment I'll need for a venture like that. . .alas, no."

"But you can't just walk away from it. Not after you've worked so hard all these years."

"I won't walk away forever, Lass. Just until I pull together the funds I need to see me through. Get some investors, perhaps. That vein of silver has waited for me this long. It won't be so bad for either of us to wait a little longer."

Jenny stared at him, turning the information over in her mind. "What do you plan to do?"

"Drive a wagon, haul adobe bricks, whatever happens to come along. I'm not too proud to do any honest work. If the good Lord intends for me to see this thing through, He'll provide a way; of that I'm sure. And in the meantime, I've heard of a young man who's worked with the mines up Colorado way. I may just strike up an acquaintance with him and see what advice he might have for me."

Jenny's long-ingrained suspicions kicked in. "Don't you go telling a total stranger about this, Red Dwyer. Do you hear me? You're a kind, honorable man and you think everyone else is the same way. But I'm here to tell you, people are capable of putting on a good front when they're after something. It isn't safe to give your trust to just anyone."

Red listened to her tirade, then fixed her with a shrewd glance mingled with a look of compassion. "I have the feeling you're speaking from experience, Jenny dear. Someday, maybe you'd like to turn the tables and be telling me your story for a change."

Jenny forced a tight smile. "Some things are better left forgotten, Red." She heard the sharpness in her voice and softened her tone. "But thank you for caring."

"I have no daughter of my own. It's easy to care about you. And anytime that burden from your past gets too heavy to bear, remember you can always share it with your old friend, Red, will you?"

Jenny gave a brief nod, her mind already on other matters. "You mentioned getting investors. How much money do you think you'd need?"

Red pulled a slip of paper and a stub of pencil from his pocket and began jotting down figures. When he'd tallied them, he pushed the paper across to her.

Jenny drummed a light tattoo on the table with her fingertips. Her earnings from the restaurant had surpassed her fondest expectations, but after the purchase of her house, she couldn't come up with the full amount Red needed.

Still, what she could manage might be enough to make a difference. She'd seen Elizabeth take a similar chance on some of the miners around Prescott and knew the potential for profit existed. Perhaps investing in Red would be a way of helping both him and herself. If Evan could be involved in more than one moneymaking enterprise, so could she.

"What if I grubstaked you half of that?" The look of surprise in his eyes made her glad she'd asked.

"Girl, I'm not asking you to part with your hard-earned money. That wasn't my intention at all."

"I know." Jenny grinned. "If I'd thought you were asking, I might not have offered." She stood and brushed the wrinkles out of her apron. "There aren't many people in this world that I trust, Red. You're one of them." She extended her hand across the table. "If you're willing to take it, the money is yours."

Red hesitated only a moment, then scraped his chair back and stood facing her. "I've traveled halfway around the world, and I've met precious few people willing to take that kind of chance on me." His hand enveloped hers in a tight grip. "You won't lose out on this, Lass. I promise. This strike will bring in enough to set us up for the rest of our days, wait and see."

# six

A flicker of doubt smote Jenny. Had she just made the blunder of a lifetime? She searched Red's eyes and found reassurance there. He was older and his appearance more grizzled, but in many ways he reminded her of Elizabeth's husband, Michael. She knew her trust hadn't been misplaced.

And if the promised wealth of the mine didn't materialize? It didn't matter. The Pueblo would continue to bring in money, and if she lost every cent of this investment, so be it. Some things were worth more than money. Friendship was one of them.

The door swung open behind her, and she turned to see Evan step inside. She shot a quick glance at Red, hoping he would understand her unspoken plea to keep their agreement just between the two of them.

"It's a quiet evening," she said, waving at the empty tables. "Any idea where all our customers have gone?"

"I do indeed." Evan let out a sharp bark of laughter. "A fistfight broke out between a couple of freighters, Maddox and Stewart. Half the men in town are standing on the sidelines, waiting to see how it turns out."

He grinned at Jenny's obvious concern. "Don't worry. The way Stewart is looking, the whole thing will be over in a matter of moments and you'll be deluged with hungry customers. And I haven't done so badly for myself, either."

"What do you mean?" Jenny had started for the kitchen to prepare for the onslaught, but Evan's last words brought her to a halt.

He slicked back his hair with both hands. "Anytime a match is even enough that the outcome is in doubt, men will be willing to bet their last dollar on the result. My job is to make sure as much of that loose cash as possible flows from their pockets into mine."

"Meaning?"

"Meaning that I covered a good many of the bets that were placed this afternoon." Evan wore a self-satisfied expression. "But I backed Maddox, not Stewart. I once saw him hit a stubborn ox and bring it to its knees."

He lifted one eyebrow at Jenny. "And what's behind that disapproving schoolmarm expression that's just settled on your face?" he asked, his voice tinged with amusement.

Jenny pressed her lips together and chose not to answer.

"Don't look so glum," Evan said. "I'm going back now to collect the profits of an afternoon well spent. Give me a little time to console the losers and send them this way. You'll have enough trade come through the door to make the cash box ring."

Jenny watched him stroll back outside, trying to control her temper.

"Are you all right, Lass?"

She spun around at the sound of Red's quiet voice. "I'm fine," she told him, hoping the smile she pasted on her lips looked sincere. Not for the world would she admit she'd been so distraught by Evan's revelation she'd forgotten her friend's presence.

Red stepped toward her, sharp lines of concern etched on his forehead. "You wouldn't be giving me a little blarney of your own, would you now? A few minutes ago, I saw trust and confidence in your eyes." He shook his head slowly. "It isn't there now."

"I'm just thinking ahead, trying to plan how to meet the demands of a herd of hungry customers arriving all at once." Her laugh didn't ring true, even to her own ears.

She hurried toward the kitchen, but Red held up his hand to stop her.

"I know you're busy, and I'll only be taking a moment more of your time." He paused and wet his lips. "I don't know what's happened to put such doubt about people in that sweet head of yours, but I want you to know there's someone else you can trust and talk to when I'm not around."

Jenny gave him a puzzled look. "Who are you talking about?"

"God."

*Oh, no. Not you, too.* She forced a bright smile to her lips and headed toward the kitchen door. "Trying to figure out how I'm going to cook, clean, and take orders from this mob all at the same time, I just wish I had someone I could trust enough to come in and do some odd jobs for me." The door swung shut behind her, cutting off Red's reply.

Jenny leaned her elbows on the counter and pressed her knuckles against her forehead. First Elizabeth, now Red. She cared for both of them and counted them as friends, something that didn't come easily for her. In every way, she had found them worthy of her trust.

If only they could be content to be her friends without having to bring God into it! She had already endured enough of Elizabeth's heartfelt pleading and assurances of God's love. Now Red had gotten into the act.

Who would have dreamed the feisty miner was of the same bent as Elizabeth and Michael? Maybe she shouldn't be surprised, though. He had the same steady look, the same calm assurance.

An assurance that could never be hers. She cupped her face in her palms, surprised to find her cheeks damp with unbidden tears. She dashed them away with the backs of her hands. Why couldn't her friends enjoy the benefits of their faith without having to emphasize the difference between them and her? Bad enough that her life had been torn apart by forces beyond her control. She didn't need to be reminded of the existence of a love she could never hope to share.

She slid a pan of biscuits into the oven, glad she had made

an extra large batch that afternoon. From what Evan said, business ought to be booming in just a few minutes.

Evan. She heard his rumbling chuckle again, as though he stood beside her in the kitchen. So he found her distaste for gambling amusing? The unwanted tears stung her eyes again and she blinked them back. Let him laugh! She had seen enough of that vice in the dim cavern of the Nugget Saloon to last her a lifetime.

Faro, monte, poker—she'd watched grim-faced men playing all of them, seen the way the lure of unearned riches drew them farther and farther into its web. She checked the biscuits, trying to shake off her black mood. How had only a month at the Nugget made such a deep impression on her?

Was it there the seeds of distrust planted by her disreputable guardian took root? She didn't know and didn't care to ponder the matter. As she had told Red, some memories were better left alone.

But the question kept niggling at her. Had she become so hardened she was now incapable of giving her trust to anyone? Surely not. Look at Michael and Elizabeth. They had won her unqualified devotion two years before, and she considered them her dearest friends.

And then there was Red. Although she'd known him only a short time, something about him inspired the same kind of confidence.

*And whom do you trust besides those three, Jenny Davis?* She brushed the bothersome thought aside. Getting the restaurant set up and running had consumed her every waking moment. She hadn't gotten to know many people in Tucson yet. When the time was right, she would make more friends.

What about Evan? Surely their business partnership counted for something. She wouldn't have pulled up stakes and come to an unknown part of the territory with someone undependable, would she? His penchant for gambling aside,

Evan had proven himself an astute businessman. She had made a good choice with him, as well.

There. Four people on her list of those she trusted didn't seem quite so bleak. Maybe she was making more progress than she'd thought.

And maybe someday she'd find someone she could believe in as wholeheartedly as Elizabeth trusted Michael. Red's company helped fill the void she felt without the O'Roarkes close at hand, and Jenny felt grateful for that.

Still, it would be nice to have a special someone in her life. Someone she could share her dreams and innermost thoughts with. Someone who could make her feel protected and safe.

She checked the biscuits one more time and pulled them from the oven. Could Evan possibly be the one? Jenny closed her eyes and tried to picture him in that role. The face that swam before her eyes, though, didn't belong to Evan Townsend.

Instead, she saw a rugged face, a firm jaw. Sandy hair she longed to smooth back with her fingertips. . .keen blue eyes that stared at her with an intensity that left her breathless. . .

The face she saw all too often in her dreams. The face of a man she'd never even spoken to: the stranger from Prescott.

Even though she had caught only a fleeting glimpse of him before he strode out of Elizabeth's restaurant, his features had been imprinted on her memory. She traced her finger along the countertop. Could he possibly be as wonderful as he had seemed from that one fleeting glance?

Her finger bumped the hot pan of biscuits, jolting her out of her reverie. She popped the wounded digit into her mouth, glad to have something to distract her attention from her daydream. Her finger throbbed, but she didn't mind the pain.

She deserved to be caught up short. It wasn't like her to allow her guard to drop like that. The stinging reminder served her right.

Of course he wouldn't be as wonderful as her imagination had played him up to be. She had built him up into some kind of fanciful hero based on nothing but fragments of an overheard conversation. Men like that didn't really exist. Not for her, at least.

The front door banged back against the wall, and footsteps clattered into the dining room. Jenny cast a practiced glance around the kitchen to make sure everything was ready and went out to greet her guests. It sounded like Evan's predicted crowd of diners had arrived at last.

❧

Another morning, another day's worth of chores. Jenny carried the last of the breakfast dishes back to the kitchen and added them to the stack on the counter. She pressed her hands against the small of her back and twisted this way and that, trying to loosen the kinks in her muscles.

Evan was right. She couldn't keep on doing everything on her own much longer.

"Where are you, Lass?" The familiar voice echoed in the dining room.

"I'll be right with you, Red." She wiped a stray smear of gravy off her fingers and hurried out, smiling at the surge of pleasure she felt at the prospect of her friend's company.

She pushed open the swinging door and stopped short when she saw Red standing with his arm draped across the shoulders of a small boy.

"What's this? Or, rather, who is this?" She softened the abrupt question with a smile and leaned down to extend her hand to the lad.

"Meet Manuel, Jenny. Manuel Ochoa, to be exact. He's the answer to your problems."

The dark-haired boy bowed over her hand with grave solemnity. *"Buenos dias, Señorita."* Then he looked up and a bright grin lit his face. "Good morning. You see? I speak English. I learn from some of the American storekeepers."

Jenny's own smile widened in response. "Good morning, Manuel. I'm pleased to meet you." She straightened and looked at Red, puzzled. "Now what's this about Manuel being the answer to my problems?"

Red's grin matched Manuel's for brilliance. "You said last night you needed someone to do odd jobs. Well, I found him for you."

Jenny felt her forehead pucker and tried to keep her smile from fading. "Red, could I talk to you for a moment?" She gestured to a spot across the room. "Excuse us, Manuel."

She led the way to a corner of the dining room and turned so her back was toward the boy. "What's going on?" she asked in a low tone. "I meant someone who could clean the tables and floors and maybe help take orders. He's just a little boy."

Red's left eyelid lowered in a conspiratorial wink. "Don't you be worrying about that now. I've known Manuel since he was just a wee tyke. He's a fine lad and a hardworking one. He'll do a grand job for you."

"But he can't be more than eight or nine," Jenny protested.

"Why don't you ask him?" Red gestured toward the middle of the room, where Manuel stood.

"I don't believe I'm letting you talk me into this," Jenny muttered.

"You trust me, Lass, remember?"

"I did up to now," she retorted, then strode back to the boy. "Manuel, how old are you? I must have someone who'll be able to do hard work."

"I am eleven." The youngster puffed out his chest and stood tall. "My cousin Rafael is bigger than me, and he is only ten. But he is *perezoso, Señorita* Davis. Lazy," he translated. "I will work hard for you."

"But I'll need someone to be here most of the day," Jenny said in a gentle tone. "What about school?"

The light in Manuel's eyes dimmed, but he kept the smile determinedly in place. "I do not go to school. My mother needs me to help bring in more money to care for the rest of my family."

"What about your father?"

The boy lifted his chin. "He is *muerto*. Dead. I am the man of the family now."

"He was helping to put up a building," Red whispered behind her. "The wall collapsed and landed on top of him."

Jenny looked down at the stoic little face and felt tears pool along her lower lids. She knew all too well the havoc wrought in a life when death tore a family asunder.

She knelt down to put herself on the boy's level. "Very well, Manuel. You're hired."

# seven

"I think the dining room is ready for this evening, *Señorita* Davis. Would you like to come and check before you leave for the afternoon?" Manuel stood straight and proud in the soft white shirt and dark trousers Jenny had given him to replace his cast-off clothing.

"I'll be right with you." Jenny spread a cloth over the pies she just had pulled out of the oven and followed her hired helper.

A quick survey of the room assured her all was in order. Every inch of the floor had been swept clean. Cups and silverware sat neatly at each place, ready to welcome their evening guests.

And she hadn't had to lift a finger. Jenny grinned at the thought that she would be able to leave for her siesta a good hour earlier than usual.

"Hiring you was one of the best business decisions I've made so far," she said as she walked back to check her dinner preparations once more.

"I told you I would be a hard worker." Manuel followed her into the kitchen and pinched off a bit of piecrust with an impudent grin. "Like you. You work very hard. Too hard, I think."

Jenny leaned against the counter and sighed. Did all the men in her life have to be obsessed with her workload? Even the little ones?

"I'm not working nearly as hard since you came," she reminded him.

"But still very hard." Manuel focused his gaze on a spot on the ceiling and went on in a voice oozing innocence. "I heard *Señor* Townsend talking to you about getting someone else to do the cooking."

54

Jenny thought back to her talk with Evan. They had been speaking in low voices in the kitchen at the time, with Manuel puttering about on the other side of the swinging door. *So much for a private conversation.* She shouldn't be surprised, though. She had already learned that Manuel had the ears of a cat. Nothing escaped his notice. "Not necessarily to take over all the cooking," she hedged. "Just to help me out a bit."

"My mother is a fine cook. She could be a great help." The boy looked directly at Jenny now, his face glowing with pride.

"Uh, Manuel, I don't know if that's such a good idea." At the sight of his crestfallen expression, she hastened to add, "I'm sure she's a very fine cook. But I'm looking for someone I can teach to cook the way I do. Your mother probably wouldn't want to change the way she does things."

The glow returned. "Oh, no. She would be very happy to have you teach her. She says you must be a good woman to give me a job like this. She will be honored to learn from you, just like me."

*How did we go from "she would" to "she will" in just a sentence?* Manuel had been a pleasure to work with, a joy to have around. But sharing the kitchen with a grown woman who already had years of cooking experience?

"I will bring her with me in the morning so you can meet her. You will like her very much."

"But then who will care for the rest of your family?"

"My sister Angelita, she helps with the younger ones."

Jenny sighed again, accepting the inevitable. "All right, Manuel. In the morning."

*"Bueno!"* He scampered to the door, ready to dash home and share his good news. He paused for a moment to call back over his shoulder, "And you can teach her English, too!"

Jenny stared at the boy's retreating back. She hadn't even thought about having to surmount a difference in language. Could she instruct someone in meal preparation using only hand gestures?

Another consideration came to mind: From what she'd learned from Manuel in the short time he'd been there, she had pieced together the story of the Ochoa family's meager existence after Mr. Ochoa's death. Manuel's mother needed all the help anyone could give her.

Elizabeth had helped Jenny when she was in dire straits. This could be Jenny's opportunity to rescue someone else, to be the one helping rather than the one in need for a change.

At any rate, thanks to Manuel, it seemed she had already committed herself.

*Jenny Davis, what have you gotten yourself into?*

❧

"This is my mother. Her name is Jacinta Ochoa. She is very glad to be here." Manuel wore a formal expression as he made the introductions and indicated the quiet woman at his side.

His mother gave Jenny a shy smile.

Jenny took in the woman's smooth complexion and slender figure. Too slender. Manuel had been eating some of his meals at the restaurant. She made a mental note to be sure Jacinta got her share of food, too. And she could send extra food home with the two of them at the end of each day. Tell them it was part of their pay, perhaps.

She smiled and tried not to let her misgivings show. "I'm happy to meet you, Jacinta. Would you like to see the kitchen now?"

The dark-eyed woman continued to smile but didn't move an inch. Manuel spoke a few words in Spanish, and his mother bobbed her head eagerly.

Jenny swallowed hard and led the way to the back of the restaurant. "Manuel," she said out of the corner of her mouth, "doesn't your mother speak *any* English?"

Manuel fairly skipped along in his excitement. "Only a word or two. But you and I, we will teach her."

Jenny almost envied Elizabeth her ability to meet all her problems with prayer. If she thought God would listen to her, surely this would qualify as a time to call upon the Almighty.

"Today we're making biscuits to go with the stew." She waited while Manuel relayed her meaning to his mother in a flurry of Spanish words. Jacinta nodded and smiled. Jenny groaned inwardly. At this rate, it would take all day just to explain one simple recipe.

Jenny mixed the ingredients, keeping up a running commentary while Jacinta watched, hoping her pupil would remember items and amounts. She stirred the mixture together and turned the dough out on a floured board.

"Next, we knead the dough." She pressed the heels of her hands against the ball of dough, turned the mass a quarter turn, folded it over, and pressed again.

Jacinta reached for the doughy ball, then copied her actions. "*Así?*"

"Like that?" the ever helpful Manuel translated.

"Exactly like that." Jenny watched the way Jacinta continued the process with her capable hands. Maybe lack of a common language wouldn't be such a problem after all.

Jacinta looked up, awaiting her next instructions.

"Now we pinch off the biscuits and pat them into circles." Jenny did the first one, then stepped back and motioned for the other woman to try her hand at it.

Jacinta pulled off a large glob of dough.

"A little smaller, perhaps," Jenny said, demonstrating again.

"Ah." A smile of comprehension lit Jacinta's face and she formed the next biscuit perfectly.

"That's right," Jenny told her. When Jacinta only looked puzzled, she added, "Good. *Bueno.*"

Jacinta spoke rapidly to Manuel. "She wants to know if you want her to go ahead and finish the biscuits on her own," he told Jenny.

She hesitated only a moment. Jacinta seemed to have the hang of it. Maybe the best thing she could do was show trust in her new employee. If disaster struck, she would only be a few yards away. "That will be fine," she said. "I'll be in the office if you need me."

⁂

Before the week was out, any misgivings Jenny had about adding a second member of the Ochoa family to the payroll had vanished like early morning dew in the Tucson sun.

Jacinta had shown a marked ability to assimilate Jenny's cooking methods and work on her own with little supervision. With only minimal help from Jenny, she had taken over the breakfast preparations and much of the lunch duties, as well.

Her cooking and Manuel's work in the dining room left Jenny free to spend several hours a day in her office, time she spent going over the books, drawing up supply orders, and making plans.

Above all, making plans. She set her pen down on the desk and propped her chin on one hand, staring dreamily through the sheer muslin curtains.

Only months before, she'd been working at Elizabeth's restaurant for little more than her room and board. Just a couple of months ago, she had to brace herself every time she ventured out into the streets of Prescott, steeling herself for a possible onslaught of cutting remarks.

In that short time, she had gone from feeling like an outcast to enjoying life as a respected member of the community and earning her own living, a good one at that. What a difference the choice to relocate to Tucson had made!

She stood and walked to the window, staring out at the scene of burgeoning growth. Two years after replacing Prescott as the territorial capital, Tucson was shedding its image as a sleepy Mexican village where travelers dreaded traversing the crooked, filthy streets, and emerging as a city worthy of its new status.

Jenny folded her arms and leaned against the window frame.

She and Tucson had a lot in common. Both had rough beginnings and times they'd prefer to forget. But both had been given a second chance, an opportunity to shake off the dust of the past and move ahead into a bright new future.

*Speaking of the future. . .* Jenny returned to her chair and picked up her pen again. If she could finish the sketches showing her plans for expansion, she could show them to Evan, along with her new ideas for the menus. Jacinta had shown her gratitude for her job and Jenny's cooking lessons by teaching Jenny to prepare some of her own favorite foods. If Evan agreed, Jenny planned to add several Mexican dishes to their menu, starting next week.

She rolled the pen between her fingers, delighting in the way things had come together. She had a home of her own, the restaurant was thriving, and even now Red was out on his new claim setting things in motion to further secure their futures. Jenny smiled. What would Red think of the changes that had come about since he brought Manuel to the Pueblo?

Voices rumbled in the outer room, signaling the arrival of the first lunch customers. Gathering up paper, pen, and ink, she carried the lot to a table in the far corner of the dining room. Seldom occupied unless they had an overabundance of diners, it made an ideal place to do work on her ledger and still interact with her patrons.

"There is mail for you, *Señorita* Davis." Manuel appeared at her elbow, a wrinkled envelope in his hand. "*Señor* Townsend left it here a little while ago."

"Evan was in here and didn't stop by the office?" Her initial pang of disappointment was quickly replaced by irritation. If Evan had time to visit with Manuel, he could have given her at least a few moments. She could have outlined her plans to him and gotten his initial reaction.

No, maybe it was better to complete the plans before showing them to him at all. He would probably be more likely to agree to them if he could see the whole picture at once.

Swallowing her frustration, she squared the stack of papers and got ready to get back to work. The envelope Manuel had left on the corner of the table caught her attention, and she picked it up, smiling when she saw the return address. She could always make time for one of Elizabeth's chatty letters.

She tore the envelope open, eager to read her friend's news.

*Dear Jenny,*

*I hope this finds you well and your business thriving. What a wonderful success you've made of it! To all the excitement of your accomplishments, I'll add one caution, and I'm sure you can guess what it is: Give God a place in your life. Despite what you think, He does love you and longs for you to be His child. You know how often I've prayed for this, how much I desire to see it happen, so I won't belabor the point. But as much contentment as you think your life holds now, it does not begin to compare with the joy and peace that can be yours when you make God your partner in life.*

*Enough of my sermonizing for now. There is excitement aplenty in the O'Roarke household these days. Can you guess? After nearly two years, Michael and I have learned we are going to be parents. I am thrilled and terrified, all at once! The responsibility of rearing a child makes the day-to-day responsibilities of running a restaurant seem trivial in comparison.*

*I have one more exciting bit of news to impart. You know that my sister Carrie keeps me informed of the happenings back East. Her last letter was full of welcome news. It seems that just a few weeks ago, Susan B. Anthony and Elizabeth Cady Stanton organized the National Woman Suffrage Association with the goal of seeking an amendment to the U.S. Constitution. Imagine, Jenny. It may not be much longer before American women get the vote!*

*How I wish you could be here with me during these thrilling days, my dear friend. But I know you have made a new home for yourself in Tucson and I would not begrudge you that for anything. And we have already shared a number of exciting times together. As always, I will continue to keep you in my prayers.*

*With love,*
*Elizabeth*

A shadow fell across the table, and Jenny looked up to see a thin, hatchet-faced man standing beside her. "Afternoon, Miss." He dipped his head and gave her a friendly smile. "I needed to speak to Townsend, but I don't see him anywhere around."

"He was here earlier," Jenny replied. "I'm not sure whether he'll be back later today or not. May I give him a message?"

"You can give him this, if you don't mind." He reached inside his broadcloth coat and drew out an envelope. Placing it on the table, he gave another nod and turned to leave.

"Whom shall I say it's from?" Jenny called after him.

He stopped in the doorway and gave her a slow wink. "Don't worry. He'll know."

Jenny slid the missive under her pile of sketches and scanned Elizabeth's letter once more before folding it and replacing it in its envelope.

A smile curved her lips. How like Elizabeth to be as excited about the new strides being made toward women's suffrage as she was about the prospect of motherhood.

*They'll make wonderful parents.* Jenny could easily picture her friends in their new roles. Elizabeth would provide firm but loving guidance and the assurance her children could do whatever they set their minds to. And Michael, with his quick sense of humor and protective spirit, would be sure his family was well cared for. Their children would grow up in a loving home, full of warmth and happiness.

The thought brought memories of her own childhood to Jenny's mind, and a leaden feeling filled her chest.

She took a deep breath, trying to sweep the sensation away, remembering that Elizabeth's letters always brought mingled joy and pain. Joy at hearing from someone she loved like a sister; pain at the reminder of the dark time in her life—the reason she'd fled Prescott in the first place.

She made a few tentative marks on her sketches, then swept the papers into a heap and carried them back to her office. Right now, she should go help Jacinta with lunch. Anything requiring concentration would have to wait until later.

# eight

"If the new wing is added over here," Jenny extended the lines indicating the north and south walls of the dining room, "and we brought the kitchen out this far," she sketched in the larger area, "then we could make an archway in the existing east wall and have room for at least six more tables." She scribbled a line where the prospective archway would be and made a few quick slashes to indicate the new exterior walls.

She looked at her drawing with a critical eye, trying to spot any weak points Evan might notice. There might be some, she decided, but she couldn't begin to spot them tonight, tired as she was.

She stretched her arms wide and rolled her head from side to side. The lamp sputtered, almost out of oil. Jenny glanced at the clock, surprised at the lateness of the hour. She had worked on the details of her plan instead of taking her usual siesta, then worked on them further after the restaurant closed for the night.

Jenny hurried to undress and get into bed before the lamp gave out completely. The late hours and extra work would be worth it, though, when she convinced Evan it would be in their best interests to spend the money to enlarge their building.

She curled on her side and watched the edge of the curtain dance in the light breeze. Her eyelids drifted closed, and she forced them open again. She needed to stay awake long enough to plan for tomorrow.

In the morning, she would make a final copy of her plan, free of scribbles and extraneous lines. When Evan came in, she would present the idea to him. If he took to it right away, they could begin construction immediately, maybe even as early as next week.

She snuggled deeper into her pillow, allowing her muscles to relax. Her lids drooped shut again, and this time they didn't open.

≥

The nightmare began as it always did. Jenny recognized it for what it was, even as it pulled her into its own distorted reality.

Harsh voices grated in her ears. Rough hands grabbed her and dragged her off, away from the shelter of Elizabeth's restaurant, no matter how she pleaded and struggled.

Someone lifted her, then dropped her onto the bed of a wagon. Her body slammed against the unyielding wood. A coarse burlap sack was forced over her head, past her shoulders, then tied shut beneath her feet. She lay alone in the darkness, with only the hated voices to keep her company.

More unpleasant sensations: bouncing, jostling, feeling new bruises form every time the wagon wheels lurched in and out of another deep rut.

*It's the dream, nothing more. It isn't real.* Jenny called on every bit of willpower she possessed to shake off the terror. Experience had taught her that if she could jolt herself awake, she could escape at this point while the images remained hazy. Some nights she managed to evade the dream before it re-created memories that were all too real.

Tonight would not be one of them. She felt herself sinking deeper into the nightmare, reliving the memories she tried to avoid in the daylight.

The wagon finally ceased its relentless jarring. Relief at that bit of respite ended with her burlap prison being dragged across the wagon bed, then lifted like a sack of meal. Footsteps plodded across the ground, then thudded across a plank floor. The sack, with Jenny in it, was dumped none too gently on the boards. She waited for what would come next.

"So what'll you do with her, now that you have her back?"

That high-pitched voice always started the conversation in her dream, just as it had the night she had been abducted by Martin Lester, the guardian who had betrayed her father's trust and traded her to the owner of the Nugget Saloon.

Liquid sloshed, and she heard a series of noisy gulps before the other voice replied, "I don't know. I can't take her back into town. That nosy biddy she's staying with will have everyone all stirred up, looking for her."

Even in her sleep, Jenny flinched at the sound of Burleigh Ames's voice. Singing for his customers at the Nugget had kept her from a worse fate, but Burleigh had plans to force her into a life she wanted no part of. Plans that had seemed all too likely to succeed until Michael O'Roarke helped her escape and find safety with Elizabeth.

And now the two men she feared most had her in their power again.

Boots scraped across the floor. One prodded her shoulder through the sacking. "She thinks she's too almighty good for the fellows in the saloon." It was Ames, then. "They want a girl who's willing, not one who'll spit in their eye. Some bill of goods you sold me, Lester. At least you got a load of whiskey out of the deal. I need a way to get my investment back."

The bottom of the bag jerked upward, and her feet lifted off the floor. In a moment, the cord holding the sack shut had been loosened.

"What are you doing?" Lester queried.

Ames dropped the end of the bag. Jenny's feet fell back to the hard floor. "Getting her out where I can look at her." His hand seized the upper end of the bag and yanked, tumbling her out onto the floor in a heap.

Jenny sat blinking in the sudden light, staring up at the menacing figures. Two of them, one of her. She could never overpower them on her own. But she'd die trying.

"Not much to look at right now, is she?" Burleigh Ames sneered.

"Oh, I don't know." Martin Lester circled her as though evaluating livestock. "Once you clean her up and get some of the dirt from the wagon off her, she wouldn't be so bad. She's got a fine, full figure, if you ask me." He cackled and took another swig from the bottle. "Maybe I'll just buy her back and keep her for myself."

Derisive laughter rumbled from Ames's barrel chest. "You had your chance with her before, and she was too much for you, remember? You'd never dare turn your back or go to sleep with her around." His face turned serious once more. "I'm the one who's losing out here. You already drank up the whiskey I traded you for her. I've got to get some kind of return for all my time and trouble."

Lester pursed his lips and eyed Jenny from head to toe with a look that made her skin crawl. "What about selling her again?"

"Who to?" Ames scoffed. "The whole town will be out looking for her."

"I'm not talking about anyone around town." Lester's voice held a crafty note. "What about selling her down in Mexico? Or trading her to the Indians?"

"Yeah." Ames drew the word out. He pondered the idea a moment longer. "Yeah, that'd work."

Jenny felt the blood drain from her face. She sat rigid, too paralyzed by fear to jump up and make a run for the door. She was done for. There would be no escape from the awful fate Lester outlined. They had won, and their victory would be her utter ruin.

"God, are You there?" She barely breathed the words aloud. "Why don't You help me?"

She jerked awake and lay in the half state between dream and reality, still whispering the words: "Are You there, God? Are You there?"

Then full awareness came, and she shuddered with sobs, using her light sheet to mop the tears from her face. She knew the answer to her questions all too well: Yes, God was there. . .for people good enough to merit His help.

But Jenny Davis wasn't one of them.

She turned her sodden pillow over and settled her cheek against the dry side. Loneliness washed over her in a wave. It would have been better if she'd been massacred along with the rest of her family. She wouldn't have to face this overwhelming sense of isolation, something she managed to ignore during her busy days but that came back to haunt her during the night hours.

If Elizabeth and Michael hadn't appeared like avenging angels, setting her free from her captors, where would she be now? She remembered sobbing in Elizabeth's arms after her rescue. "You came! I was all alone, but you came for me!" The wonder of being sought after, of being loved so much still hadn't left her, even after all this time.

Elizabeth had held her close and whispered, "But you weren't alone, Dear. God was with you and kept you safe."

Jenny shook her head violently against the pillowcase, just as she had in Elizabeth's arms back then. If God had been with her, she would never have been taken captive in the first place, never have had to hear Martin Lester's derisive cackle or read the evil intent in Burleigh Ames's eyes.

Maybe God indeed led Michael and Elizabeth to the isolated cabin where she had been held prisoner. But if that were the case, it was because He cared about their distress, not hers.

She curled into a ball and pulled the sheet up tight around her shoulders. Rescue. Michael and Elizabeth had saved her that night, protected her from who knows what unspeakable end. But they were back in Prescott, and neither they nor anyone else could protect her now from the memories that threatened to undo her.

She drew her knees up tight against her chest. If only another strong protector would come into her life. Someone who would care for her and shield her from whatever dangers might come her way. Someone like her imaginary hero, who guarded the rights of others.

Her wistful laugh floated out into the darkness. That wasn't going to happen, and well she knew it. She would have to find another way to fill the empty longing deep inside her.

Wrapping her arms around her knees, she rocked back and forth, hoping sleep would claim her soon, sleep without dreams this time. The nightmare would come again, but please, not tonight.

If there was any mercy, not tonight.

# nine

"Set it against that wall, please. And the desk goes over there, near the window." Jenny stepped back to give the struggling workmen space to maneuver the heavy pieces of furniture around in her small living room.

When they had placed the pieces to her satisfaction, Jenny closed the door behind them and looked around with delight. The serpentine-back sofa might look somewhat out of place against the rough adobe walls, but a few strategically placed wall hangings would soften the contrast.

And the desk! Jenny ran her fingers along the gleaming walnut surface and marveled at its satiny feel. She rolled the cylinder top back into its compartment to expose the writing surface, then slid it closed again.

It seemed a shame for Ambrose Long's belongings to be sold off when he died, but his widow needed money to live on once she returned to the States. She had obviously hated parting with her treasured furnishings, but she'd been happy enough to see Jenny as the new owner. "It comforts me to know they'll be appreciated," she put it.

Jenny lowered herself gently onto the sofa's delicate upholstery. To think that such elegance could be hers. And that she'd been able to afford it! The heavy furniture took up most of the space in the room. Jenny didn't mind; it gave the place a sense of solidity.

She went into her bedroom and stripped off the comforter, sheets, and pillow. The workmen would have to take care of moving the bed itself when they brought the Longs' maple spool bed later that afternoon.

Jenny eyed the dimensions of the room, hoping she hadn't

misjudged the size of her new bed. It would be a tight fit, but surely they could squeeze it in. She wouldn't have much space left to move around, but it wouldn't matter when that wonderful bed would be hers. These new furnishings filled her house, making it more of a home, and gave her much pleasure. If only she could find something that would fill the void in her heart as easily.

*಄*

"Good morning, Jenny. Miss me?" Evan tossed his hat toward the corner of the office, where it settled neatly onto a peg.

"Morning? More like early afternoon." Jenny rose from her work with the ledger and faced him, her hands planted on her hips. "How can you stroll in here after being gone for five days straight with nothing more than a casual 'Morning, did you miss me'?"

A bright smile played across Evan's face. "You did miss me, then."

"I was worried, Evan. Worried sick! You were supposed to be back days ago. Where have you been all this time?"

He took off his jacket and draped it casually across the corner of the desk. "Working, my dear. And I've pulled in a good profit for my efforts."

Jenny narrowed her eyes. "Gambling, you mean. What town have you left poorer this time?"

"Ah, Jenny. You're beginning to sound more like a disapproving wife than a business partner." Evan chuckled and lifted her chin with his forefinger, a gesture that never failed to make her feel like a backward child. "When you agreed to come down here, I warned you I might not be around all the time."

"All the time?" She pulled away from him and folded her arms across her chest. "You're gone more than you're here. And it's what you're doing when you're gone that concerns me. You know how I feel about gambling."

He perched on the edge of the desk and grinned at her,

unabashed. "I told you the day we met that I'm first and foremost a businessman, and it's true. Gambling is my business. It's the way I finance my other ventures, and I'm good at it. Very, very good. Now what is it you've been waiting to talk to me about these five long days?"

Jenny let out a huff of disgust but turned to pull her sketches of the proposed expansion from the desk drawer. It was impossible to pin Evan down about his behavior when he was in one of these playful moods. Better to swallow her irritation and get his approval of her plans while he seemed in a frame of mind to listen.

"I wanted to show you a few of my ideas and see what you think." She spread the papers out on the desk, and Evan stood to look at them.

"What's that?" Evan asked, pointing at the corner of an envelope that protruded from under one of the sheets.

"I have no idea." Jenny picked it up and recognition came to her. "Oh, I nearly forgot. A man left it with me to give to you a few days ago. Five days ago, to be exact," she added, unable to resist driving the point home once more. "The day you took off without a word." She wagged the envelope underneath Evan's nose.

He snatched it out of her hand, tapped her on the head with it, and tucked it inside his coat pocket without a second glance. "All right, consider it delivered. Your duty is done, Jenny dear. Your hardworking, Puritan soul can relax." He laughed outright at her look of distaste. "Now tell me about these plans of yours before you burst."

A half hour later, Evan still remained bent over the drawings. Jenny tiptoed past the office door for the tenth time in as many minutes and peered inside, trying to gauge his reaction.

"He is still there?"

She whirled at the unexpected voice. "Manuel!" she scolded. "You shouldn't sneak up on me like that."

"I did not sneak, *Señorita* Davis. You just did not hear me coming." His teeth flashed when he smiled. "There is a difference."

Jenny felt the corners of her lips tug upward. "I suppose you have a point," she said. "And the answer to your question is yes. He's still looking at the plans."

"Actually, he's finished looking." Evan's voice made them both jump, then laugh sheepishly. "Jenny, would you come inside? I'd like to discuss these with you. And you. . ." He pointed to Manuel. "You will find something to do besides listening at the door, understood?"

"*Sí.*" Manuel showed no offense at the mild rebuke. "It is time to help my mother clean the kitchen before siesta."

"That boy's an incorrigible eavesdropper," he said, his crooked grin belying the stern words.

"He's an absolute delight," Jenny retorted, mirroring his smile. "And I don't know how I got along without him. Or Jacinta, either. He's bright, hardworking, and always here when I need him. Unlike some other person I could mention."

Evan raised his hands in surrender. "I give up. Point taken, message noted. I shall keep you apprised of my whereabouts from here on out. Will that satisfy you?"

"It will do for a start." Jenny tossed her head back, trying to cover the sudden nervousness that swept over her. What did he think about her plans?

"I've gone over your drawings and the lists you've come up with," he began. He stirred through the stack of papers with his forefinger, then looked straight at her. "And I must say I'm tremendously impressed."

Jenny let out a whoosh of air and he chuckled. "Nervous, were you? You needn't have been. You've done a very thorough job here. There's plenty of room on the property to make the changes you've suggested, and these lists you've made. . ." He lined up three sheets of paper along the desktop and shook his head admiringly.

"These are what decided me," he said, pointing to each

sheet in turn. "You've given me a list of materials and their cost, the number of meals we can expect to serve in the new setup, and the overall profit we'll realize by carrying this out. If you needed a loan and I were a banker, I'd give you the money without a qualm."

"Then you agree we should do it?" Jenny's feet wanted to dance a jig across the floor. "When can we start?"

"How does next week sound?" Evan asked. "Assuming I can get the materials and workers lined up by then, of course."

"Wonderful!" Jenny clapped her hands. "And we'll be able to keep right on serving meals during most of the construction, too. Look, I've made some notes here." She riffled through the stack and pulled out another sheet.

Evan waved the paper away. "I'll take your word for it. I am thoroughly convinced you could have designed the Great Pyramids and drawn up the plans to do them. If you say it's feasible, that's good enough for me."

❧

"Good-bye, Jacinta, Manuel. I'll see you this evening." Jenny ushered her employees out and locked the door behind them. She meant to take part of her afternoon break time to measure and mark the east wall for the archway, and she didn't want any interruptions.

Staccato taps sounded at the door even before she turned away. Hoping it was Jacinta coming back after some forgotten item and not a customer hoping for a late lunch, she drew the bolt and opened the door a crack.

"Red!" she cried in delight. She pulled the door wide open, then paused and gave him a second look. "At least I think it's you."

The wiry miner removed his obviously brand-new hat, his clean-shaven cheeks creasing when he smiled. "Aye, it's me, Lass. All cleaned up and looking my finest. No wonder you thought it might be someone else."

Jenny shut the door when he stepped inside and turned to

inspect her friend. "Look at you! I've never seen you looking so dapper."

"That's me," Red said with a proud grin. "A regular clothes-horse. I know you're closed for business now, but I wanted to talk to you without a passel of people around. Do you have time to talk to an old miner?"

"For you, Red, I always have time."

He sauntered to his favorite table and fixed her with a mischievous gaze. "Would you be having any pie taking up space in your kitchen that you need for other things?"

Jenny laughed aloud. "How about some dried apple pie? That's your favorite, as I recall."

Red rubbed his hands together. "Excellent! That will make it seem like a party, and Jenny girl, we have cause for celebrating."

"What—"

"No, you're not going to make me get ahead of myself. I've waited long enough to spring this news on you, and I'm going to do it my own way. Go ahead and get the pie, and bring a piece for yourself, too."

Thoroughly intrigued by his tantalizing remarks, Jenny hurried to comply. "All right," she said, setting the pie plates on the table and pulling up a chair. "What's all the mystery about? You come in here looking like a fine gentleman and hinting at some great revelation. What's going on?"

Red stood and spoke in an oratorical tone. "Miss Jenny Davis, I am pleased to report that your faith in me was not in vain. You are now not only a restaurateur, but part owner of the Silver Crown silver mine."

It took a moment for the impact of his news to sink in. Jenny leaped to her feet. "You mean it's done? The claim is filed, legal and everything? The mine is yours?"

"Not mine, Lass. Ours." Red's eyes misted and he gave her a tender glance. "You gave me the help I needed to get back out there and stake the claim, and I'm not about to leave you out of the picture. You'll get back every penny of the money you invested in an old man's dream and a packet more besides."

"But I didn't mean to—"

"I know you didn't," Red cut in. "You only meant to help me out of the goodness of your heart, and that's why I want to return the favor."

Jenny's head felt light, as though she were soaring up through the clouds into the rosy dawn of a bright new day. Could this be happening to her? On top of her joy at Evan's lavish approval, the euphoria she felt was almost too much to bear.

"Are you all right?" Red's light touch on her shoulder and the lines of concern on his forehead brought her back to the moment.

"I'm fine. Just a little overwhelmed, I think. Let me get us some coffee, and you can tell me more about it."

# ten

"So what's the next step?" Jenny asked after her heartbeat had returned to a more normal pace.

Red rubbed his chin. "I've been pondering that very question. Twenty years ago, I would have looked forward to conquering the rock with my own two hands. Just me and my own strength, pitted against that vein of silver." He took a long swallow of his coffee. "But now I'm that much older. Older and a wee bit wiser, I hope. Wise enough to know that I don't have the vigor to wrest the silver out of the ground myself, nor do I have the knowledge of the best way to do it."

He picked up a crumb from his plate and popped it into his mouth. "Most of the prospecting I did in California was for gold, and all I ever had there was a placer claim. Swirling a pan through the water hoping to find a nugget or two or some gold dust in the bottom is a far cry from putting together a major silver operation." He shook his head. "I was able to find the lode, Lass, but I don't know the proper way to get at it."

Jenny furrowed her brow. "If we can't get the silver out, what good is the mine to us?"

"That's where we're going to need a third partner. Someone we can trust. Someone who understands the ins and outs of hard rock mining and can recognize the potential in what we have."

A hollow feeling settled in the region of Jenny's stomach. She should have known Red's big strike sounded too good to be true. Not wanting to burst his bubble too quickly, she asked gently, "And just where do you suppose you're going to find someone like that?"

Red slapped his palm on the table and grinned. "It's already done. Remember that fellow from Colorado I mentioned? He sounded like just the kind of man we need, so I looked him up as soon as I cleaned up a bit after I got back to town."

"Red, you didn't!" Jenny gaped at her friend. "You offered a perfect stranger a share in our mine without knowing a thing about him?"

"We spent a good bit of time visiting first. He had no idea he was talking to anything more than a fine-looking Irish gentleman." He gave her a saucy wink. "I learned all I needed to know before I said a word to him about the mine."

A feeling of despair welled up inside Jenny. "You're incorrigible, do you know that? You've only just met the man, and you're willing to trust him with the treasure you've been searching for your whole life?"

Her outburst didn't appear to have the least effect on Red's good humor. He leaned back in his chair and stretched his legs in front of him. "I've lived a good while, Lass. Not as long as some, but far longer than others. You, for instance. How is it that an old codger like me, who's traveled far and wide and seen a good bit of the sorry side of human nature, can find it in his heart to take most people on faith while a lovely young thing like yourself doles out her trust like a starving man sharing his last crumb of bread?"

The accusation hit its mark. Jenny pushed herself to her feet. "I'll just clear these dishes," she said. "I'm late getting home."

"Wait." Red's fingertips barely touched the back of her hand but had the effect of pinning it to the table. "I may be overstepping my bounds, Jenny, but let me say this anyway. You've let it slip once or twice that you've no family left. I don't know what happened to them or to you, that you're so wary of life. But it might help to unburden yourself to a friend. Let me help you carry the load, so to speak."

Jenny grew rigid, feeling as if the blood in her veins had turned to ice. No one in Tucson knew of her past. She had planned to keep it that way, let her dark secrets stay dead and buried.

She darted a quick glance at Red's face and saw only compassion in his expression. She did trust Red and counted him as her friend. Did she have enough confidence in him to share the events that altered her life forever?

The moment hung suspended in time. Red seemed in no hurry, just waited patiently for her answer. When she didn't speak, he said, "I don't mean to be treading where I shouldn't. I have no daughter of my own. If you need someone to talk to about whatever it is that's weighting your heart so, I'd consider it a privilege if you'd let me stand in for your father."

Slowly, Jenny's knees unlocked and lowered her back into her chair. A father. How she missed her own! Maybe she could let Red stand in his place, just for a bit.

"You know my family's gone," she began, surprised to find the words flowed freely now that she had decided to unloose them. "But I don't think I ever told you how it happened." She drew a deep breath. Even Elizabeth hadn't heard everything. The wounds then had been too recent, too painful.

"We had a farm several miles north of Prescott, my parents, my little brother, and me. Pa raised beans and potatoes and corn. Ma had a kitchen garden I helped her with, and we kept a couple of cows. Nothing fancy, but it was ours." Her voice softened with the memory.

"Johnny—that's my brother—wanted so much to be like our pa. He was just getting old enough to help a lot with the outdoor work, and he followed Pa everywhere." While she spoke, the scene before her shifted and she saw, not Red and the restaurant, but images of that terrible day on the farm.

"That last day, Johnny had gone out to help Pa bring in the cows. It was cold that day, and Ma was fixing a stew. She sent me out to the root cellar to dig out some potatoes.

"It wasn't really a cellar, more like a pit we'd dug out of the side of the hill near our house. We kept it covered with brush so it didn't stand out. Pa always told us if any trouble came, we were to go straight to the root cellar and stay there." Her voice caught. "It was our safe place. Except I was the only one who stayed safe."

She closed her eyes but couldn't shut out the scenes of what happened next. "They showed up without any warning: six Apaches. We knew there had been depredations to the south of us, but we hadn't been bothered. Pa said he didn't expect any trouble, but it came anyway." She wadded the fabric of her skirt in one hand and brushed the tears from her cheeks with the other.

"I was pulling potatoes out of the straw when I heard shouting outside. I peeked past the brush and saw Pa standing near the barn, facing north. Johnny was behind him, flattened up against the side of the barn like a scared rabbit. They yelled something at Pa, then arrows started flying and he went down. I couldn't think, couldn't move. Then two of them got down and ran over to the house. The next thing I knew, Ma was screaming. She kept begging them to let her go, to take whatever they wanted and leave us alone. Then the screams got louder. Then they just. . .stopped." She lifted one hand and let it drop helplessly in her lap.

"All I could see of Pa were his legs stretched out past the corner of the barn. He wasn't moving." She drew a shuddering sigh. "And then I saw Johnny take off like a cottontail, heading for the cabin. He got out of my line of vision, but I saw one of the Indians take off after him. A moment later, I heard Johnny cry out, and I knew he hadn't made it."

Red wiped a knuckle across his eyes and cleared his throat. "What happened next, Lass?"

"I wanted to run out there and help them, but I couldn't make myself move. I watched the Indians drive the cows and horses off and set fire to our house and the barn. And then they rode away. The next thing I remember, neighbors who'd seen the smoke came riding up and were calling my name."

Red reached across the table and tightened his fingers around hers. "I'm sorry. So sorry. You went through a horrible time." He pulled a handkerchief from his pocket and handed it to her.

She crumpled the soft cloth in her fist. "There's more." Now that she'd started, she found she wanted to unburden herself of the whole sordid story. "My father appointed a guardian for Johnny and me in case anything happened to him and our mother. I'd lost everyone I loved that day, but at least I knew I'd have a roof over my head." She dabbed at her nose with Red's handkerchief. "What I didn't know—and what Pa didn't, either—was the kind of man Martin Lester really was. He seemed happy enough to take me in. I had no idea he had other than kindly motives until he. . .started making advances."

"The blackguard!" Red's face grew dark. "Did anyone come to your aid?"

Jenny shook her head. "He had a farm a ways from ours. There weren't any near neighbors, nobody I could run to. And I didn't have the courage to take off across country on my own. Not after what happened to my family." Her voice quavered again and she cleared her throat before she went on.

"He kept me around for two months—giving me time to get adjusted to the idea, as he put it. Then he got tired of me fighting him off, and he. . ."

"What is it, Lass?" Red urged. "What did he do?"

"He bartered me," Jenny said, her voice barely above a whisper. "Traded me to a saloon keeper for a load of whiskey. He traded me, Red! Just like a horse or a piece of property." The emotional dam she had guarded for so long burst at last. Jenny lowered her head to the table and wept, violent sobs tearing at her throat.

She'd done it now. Opened the floodgate that would let the nightmare deluge her nights with terror once again. All the same, she felt a sense of relief. Red hadn't shied away or drawn back in disgust.

She heard his chair scrape across the floor, then felt him kneel beside her, stroking her hair with his calloused hands. "But it's all over now, my girl. You've gone through a terrible time, but it's behind you."

He continued stroking her head until the storm subsided. "Somehow, God delivered you from the clutches of evil men and—"

Jenny raised her head enough to prop it on her folded arms. "Not God. A man named Michael."

"Like the archangel himself!" Red's face shone with a radiant light.

"No, but he's the only man who ever cared for me as a person since my pa died." She pressed her fingertips against her swollen eyelids, then looked straight at Red. "And except for you and my pa, he's the only man I've ever trusted."

"Ah, I'm beginning to understand." Red sat back on one heel and regarded her with eyes that mirrored her own pain. "You've suffered, and so you've closed the door of your heart to anyone, for fear some miscreant will take advantage of you again."

Jenny sniffed. "I guess that about sums it up. Now you know why I can't trust anyone. Ever."

"That's where you're wrong, Lass." Red's eyes regained their sparkle. "What you need more than anything is to trust again, and trust the only One who's worthy of your confidence."

"But I do trust you, Red. I just told you so."

"Not me, Lass. I'm honored to know you feel that way, and I'll do my best to live up to your faith in me. But try as I might, there's always a chance I may let you down. I'm only human after all."

"Then who—"

"God, Jenny. He's the only one you can count on never to leave you, never to let you down."

"Not again, Red. I can't take any more of that right now." She stood and crossed the room to distance herself from

Red's quizzical look. "Don't you see? Some people are good enough for God, some aren't. I don't know how He decides, but it's obvious I'm not one He's chosen to love."

Red stared at her, then drew himself up. "If you're thinking I was born some kind of saint, you're wrong as wrong can be. Maybe next time I'll tell you some different stories of my younger days." The corner of his mouth quirked up in a half smile. "Then again, maybe I won't."

He pushed himself to his feet, moving with the stiffness of his years. "I won't keep trying to convince you. I'm not the one who can make you believe God loves you. Only the Lord Himself can do that." He settled his new hat on his head and started for the door, then turned back. "But you can know one thing for sure: I'll be praying for you."

⚓

Jenny climbed into her bed that night with Red's words echoing through her mind. She trusted him in other things; could she trust him in this as well? What if his assertion that God loved her—as impossible as that seemed—was true?

She considered the possibility. What difference would God's presence make in her life?

Jenny rolled to one side and scooted down a bit so she could see the Big Dipper through her window. God created those stars and all the rest. Did He live among them, up on some lofty plane where He could look down and consider all His works?

Supposing the Maker of the universe did decide to take her as one of His own, what then? Could she hope to feel as pure as Elizabeth and Michael, as confident in His love as Red?

What would that mean to her? She wrapped one of her long blond ringlets around her finger and pondered the concept of truly feeling clean. Teardrops gathered in the corners of her eyes at the thought of never caring what other people thought about her or her past.

If it were possible. . . But it wasn't. Reality jolted her to her senses. According to Elizabeth and Michael, God never changed. Did that mean she had imagined His love when she was a little girl gazing up at this same night sky with her mother's soft lullaby in her ears?

Wasn't He supposed to be in control of all things? Then she had to believe He allowed her family to meet such hideous deaths and her to witness it. The power to create the universe, and He hadn't lifted a finger to avert the tragedy that set her life on its cruel path. What kind of love was that?

And God was holy. She knew that much. Holiness couldn't exist in the presence of wickedness. That would most certainly include the kind of goings-on that were considered normal behavior at the Nugget Saloon. It included Jenny, herself. No matter that she'd spent her weeks there warding off advances from leering customers. No matter that she'd earned Burleigh Ames's wrath by refusing to take any of the men upstairs to her room. She had been pawed and grabbed at, despite her best efforts to protect herself. Even against her will, the groping hands had left their mark. And left her tainted.

Tainted with a stain that blemished her soul forever and left her unworthy to even think of being welcomed into God's presence. He would have to change His very nature to accept her as she was today, and God didn't change.

A low moan escaped her throat, and Jenny gathered the sheet tight under her chin despite the sweltering temperatures of the hot summer night. She couldn't bear to throw the layer of fabric back and further expose herself to the all-seeing eye of the Almighty. She closed her eyes and forced a swallow down her dry throat. She knew who she was, no getting around it. Better to accept that fact and do what she could to make her life as tolerable as possible than to dwell on what could never be.

# eleven

"And how is my lovely partner this morning?" Evan's cheerful greeting set Jenny's teeth on edge.

"Fine." She pushed open the office window to take advantage of any breeze the day might offer and forced a bright smile, well aware that she looked anything but lovely. A sleepless night as the unwilling hostess to a myriad of dark thoughts had taken care of that.

"As a matter of fact, I heard some exciting news yesterday." Maybe setting her mind on the positive things in her life would let her ignore the emptiness that threatened to engulf her these days whenever she let down her guard.

Evan sprawled in the chair and leaned his elbow against the desk. "I'm up for some excitement. What did you hear?"

"You remember Red Dwyer?"

"The scrawny little miner who looks almost as weather-beaten as his burro does?"

Jenny shot him an exasperated look. "Underneath that rough exterior, he's a gentleman through and through. I've known far too few of those."

Evan held up his left hand in a lazy gesture. "I stand admonished. Now take that scowl off your face and tell me what your little leprechaun had to say."

Excitement bubbled up inside Jenny despite her fatigue. "I grubstaked him awhile back. He came back yesterday to tell me he's located a silver strike he thinks will be very profitable. And," she added with a broad smile, "he's decided to make me his partner. I now hold an interest in a silver mine. Even if nothing comes of it, that's still a pretty thrilling thought."

"You mean the old codger actually found something

worthwhile?" Evan lowered his head and stared at the floor, then looked straight at her, his eyes snapping with enthusiasm. "If this turns out to be more than the fevered imagination of one more prospector who claims he's found the mother lode, you're going to need more partners than just the two of you."

Jenny watched him, biting back a cry of dismay. Evan always had his eye on the main chance. What could he be up to now?

"Red's a nice enough fellow," Evan continued, "but face it, he's never struck it rich before. He'd hardly know the best way to go about developing the claim, if it's anywhere near as rich as he says. And you. . ." He gave Jenny a half smile and shrugged. "You're a wonder at running this restaurant, but working a mine is a different proposition altogether. You both need someone with a more diversified background, someone with the connections to make the most of this opportunity."

Jenny directed a cool glance his way, certain she knew where this was headed. "And that someone would be. . . ?"

Evan swept his hands apart and bowed with a flourish. "I know what it takes to deal with investors, and I have the connections to make it happen." He stepped toward her, his eyes glittering. "Take me into the partnership, Jenny. I can help."

*Help whom?* She recognized the truth of the words the moment they flashed into her mind. In the time she'd known him, she'd learned one thing about Evan: His first and last motive for taking any action was based on what he considered best for Evan Townsend. Offering to help out of a spirit of altruism simply wasn't in his nature.

"I don't think so, Evan." She turned and looked out the window. "Thank you for the offer, but Red said he already has someone lined up." *Someone he barely knows and I haven't even met.* Which would be better, the stranger, who might or might not live up to Red's expectations, or Evan, whose motives she knew all too well?

Evan stepped up close behind her. "And who's this person he's taken on? What do you know about him?"

*Only that Red trusts him, however wise or foolish that may be.* She kept her misgivings to herself and lifted one shoulder. "I'm supposed to meet him soon. I'll be able to tell you more about him then."

The air Evan hissed out between his teeth stirred the ringlets against the back of her neck. "I guess I'm too late, aren't I?" He chuckled, seeming to regain his typically easygoing manner. "Let Red know about my offer, will you? The time may come when you need me, and for you, I'll be willing to step in and help."

"I'll do that," Jenny agreed, grateful for his capitulation, even more grateful when he picked up his hat and left the room.

❧

"He's coming, Jenny." Red peered through the kitchen doorway. Excitement radiated from him, making his face look like that of a child on Christmas morning. "He'll be here in just a moment."

"Who's coming?" Jenny removed four apple pies from the oven and set the heavy pan on the counter.

"Andrew Garrett," Red announced, giving the Rs a fine roll. "Our new partner," he added in answer to Jenny's blank expression.

"Oh. Oh!" What a day for Jacinta's youngest to develop croup! Jenny hadn't realized how used she'd become to being free of the cooking duties. She shut the oven door and wiped the back of her hand across her forehead. "Let me just cover these pies."

Red glanced over his shoulder and smiled. "Be out as soon as you can, Lass. He's just arrived." He hustled off toward the outer door.

Jenny quickly tossed a clean cloth over the pie pans, then thought of her appearance. "Wonderful," she muttered, smoothing back the damp strands of hair the blistering Tucson heat had left dangling along the sides of her face. "I can just imagine what I look like. If his knowledge of mines isn't any better than his timing, we are not off to a good start." At least he managed to come between the breakfast and lunch crowds. She yanked off her apron and hurried out into the dining room.

Red stood near the door in animated conversation with a tall, sandy-haired man. He beamed when he saw Jenny cross the room toward them. "Here she is now," he said to his companion. "Andrew, meet Jenny Davis, the third partner in the Silver Crown Mine."

The stranger turned and looked at Jenny with piercing blue eyes. Eyes she remembered from one brief encounter in Elizabeth's restaurant. Eyes she'd seen in her daydreams ever since.

Did he remember, too? But why should he? They had only exchanged a fleeting glance, nothing that would probably matter to him, even if the moment had branded his image in her soul.

She struggled to compose her features and forced herself to keep moving as though she didn't feel like she'd just been struck by a bolt of lightning. With her attention focused on her daydream come to life, her feet tangled in a chair leg. She scrambled for balance but succeeded only in stumbling again. With a cry of alarm, she pitched forward.

Andrew jumped forward and caught her elbow in a strong grip. A tingling shock jolted through Jenny's arm. She regained her balance and pulled away, placing the fingertips of her other hand on the arm he had touched.

Andrew seemed as affected by their contact as she did. He stared at Jenny, his gaze probing hers with a long, measuring look. "Did I hurt you?" he asked in the deep voice she remembered from Prescott.

Jenny shook her head but couldn't speak. Standing in his presence, close enough to see the details of his face, she could only stare. She drank in his appearance with her eyes, filling in the gaps her memory had missed. At the moment, she wanted nothing more than to give in to her fancies and lose herself in the blue depths of his gaze.

"You're sure you're all right, Lass?" Red's forehead bunched into a mass of fine wrinkles. "You look a wee bit shaken."

The solicitous query brought her back to her senses. "No. I mean, yes. I'm fine." Jenny tore her gaze away from Andrew and gave Red a wavering smile.

"That was quite a stumble," Andrew said. "You're certain I didn't hurt you?" He reached out as if to touch her arm again.

Jenny pulled back quickly. "I'm fine," she repeated. "Shall we sit down?"

She led the way to a table before the other members of the newly formed partnership could question her well-being again. Let them think she'd been shaken up by her near fall. Not for the world did she want them to see how close she'd just come to throwing her hard-won dignity to the wind.

Andrew hadn't hurt her, only set her emotional equilibrium spinning out of control. And that could prove just as dangerous as a physical tumble, maybe even more so. Jenny seated herself with aplomb and donned a mantle of cool reserve. She would have to be on her guard around this man.

❧

Andrew followed his new partner, trying not to show the surge of excitement he felt when he recognized her as the captivating young woman from Prescott. In the fleeting moment when their gazes had locked during their first encounter, she had left an impression that haunted his memory ever since. Rather than throwing himself into his work in Tucson with his usual fervor, he'd found himself uncharacteristically impatient, chafing at every delay. Now he understood why: His physical self had been going about his work here, all the while his mind had been set on returning to Prescott to look into those aquamarine eyes once again.

And here she was, in Tucson! Who would have thought

that joining forces with Red Dwyer would lead him to her? Why hadn't he seen her before? No matter. The important thing was that he saw her now and planned to keep on seeing her for a long time to come.

*Lord, I don't know how You managed to bring her here. Or why, for that matter. But if I enter into Your plans in that regard, I want You to know I'm more than grateful.*

He sat across the table from her to put himself in direct line with those amazing blue-green eyes. Or were they more turquoise? Her hair, too, defied a quick description. Just when he'd classified it as golden blond, a ray of sunlight streaming through the window sent copper glints shimmering through her curls.

It would take time—and a lot of study—to sort it all out. And that would be just fine with him. They would have much to talk about in getting the partnership set up. Plenty of plans to make. And knowing that Miss Jenny Davis had an interest in the mine made him all the more determined to see it succeed.

She gave Red a warm smile. "Where do we begin?"

"Ask Andrew," he replied. "He's our expert."

Jenny turned and looked straight into Andrew's eyes, and he braced himself for another heart-stopping shock. This time, though, it didn't happen. Jenny wore the same smile she'd directed at Red, but something was missing. The smile was there, but her eyes held a shuttered look, as though she'd lowered a protective shield.

"Well, Mr. Garrett, what do you suggest?" Her tone was polite but decidedly cool.

Andrew blinked and tried to get his thoughts back on track. What had just happened? Had he imagined that electric charge when he touched her? Surely she had felt it, too. He would have sworn to it only moments before. Now she looked at him as though she'd never seen him before, showing no sign of the kinship they'd seemed to share.

"I'll need to ride out to the claim with Red and give it a good looking over first. After that, I'll have a better idea of what we'll need to begin work." He hoped his inner turmoil didn't show. Trying to make sense of this situation was like chasing after a pile of dry leaves scattered by a sudden gust of wind.

An unwelcome thought struck him. Maybe she didn't remember their earlier meeting. Perhaps their connection when he touched her had been a figment of his imagination.

All right, then. He could accept that. In his mind, their acquaintance had already been of long standing, but he couldn't expect her to have the kind of feelings he'd already allowed to build up in his mind for someone she'd just met. He would have to take a few steps backward in his thinking and start afresh. He realized Jenny was speaking again and leaned forward to catch her words.

"I was talking to Evan earlier," she said to Red, the cool tone still in her voice. "He said he'd be more than willing to come into the partnership if we needed his help. I told him you already had someone in mind, but I promised I'd let you know."

"No need for that," Red replied with a grin. "We have the expertise of the esteemed Mr. Andrew Garrett on our side, and that should be quite enough." He slapped Andrew on the shoulder to punctuate his words.

"That's fine," Jenny said quietly. "I just wanted to let you know he offered."

*Who's Evan?* Andrew's mind probed the possibilities while Red went on enthusiastically about their future prospects. Could Evan be Jenny's brother? A suitor? Or worse, a fiancé? Red hadn't mentioned any such person, but that didn't mean anything. One didn't introduce a new business partner by outlining the details of his or her private life.

*Lord, I don't know who this person is, but I'm already prepared not to like him very much. Help me to keep a right attitude in this and try to see what You're doing.*

# twelve

By the time the arrival of lunch customers sent Jenny flying back to the kitchen to dish up new orders, the trio had established a beginning plan of action. Still to be decided was whether they wanted to sell shares to raise more capital. She mulled over the idea while she moved from the stove to the counter and back again.

Red was trustworthy; of that she had no doubt. Less certain was his wisdom in bringing Andrew Garrett into the partnership on such short acquaintance. The image of Andrew's face floated before her eyes while she stirred the gravy and set more bread dough out to rise.

Not until the last of the lunch customers left and she was ready to close down for the afternoon did she have a moment to herself to try to piece her scattered thoughts together. She poured herself a glass of water and sat next to an open window to catch as much of the slight breeze as she could.

What was it that Red saw in Andrew that sparked his trust? What did she herself know about Andrew Garrett? An overheard conversation and tender feelings from her daydreams didn't count, she reminded herself. She needed to know the real man, not the paragon of virtue she had built up in her mind.

His eyes were the same as she remembered. Deep blue, with a steady gaze that could make her heart stand still in her chest. That much, at least, hadn't been a product of her imagination.

And that voice. Even in memory, its rich timbre made her insides feel like melted butter. The same firm tone she had heard through Elizabeth's kitchen door in the altercation between Andrew and Earl Waggoner, the unscrupulous mining agent. She remembered Andrew's ire upon realizing Waggoner meant to bilk the miner he represented. That should count in his favor, she decided, pressing the cool glass of water against her forehead. But did one noble deed mean he could be trusted in all things?

The outside door to the office slammed. Jenny jumped and let out a little cry, her hand pressed against the base of her throat.

"Oh, are you still here?" Evan appeared in the office doorway, pushing a shock of his dark hair back off his forehead "I didn't mean to frighten you." He crossed the room and pulled up a chair close to hers, his relaxed smile putting her at ease again.

"It's all right. I just had my mind on other things."

Evan tilted his head to one side. "Thinking about your silver mine? You aren't getting ready to pull out on me, are you?"

"Hardly!" Jenny laughed. "From the discussion I had with Red and Andrew, it seems there's far more to establishing a mine than just going out and digging. It may be months, maybe even years, before we see a profit."

Evan lounged comfortably in a chair and stretched his legs out before him. "So you finally met the mystery partner, did you? What did you think of him?"

"Red seems quite taken with him," Jenny hedged, unwilling to admit her own doubts.

"That isn't much of an answer." Evan narrowed his eyes and regarded her thoughtfully. "Considering that you were ready to leave Prescott and travel here with me after only a few minutes of conversation, I'd say you're a woman capable of sizing up a person pretty quickly. If you still aren't sure of this fellow after your business discussion, that says something, doesn't it?"

Jenny evaded his gaze. "It really isn't the same."

"Did you tell Dwyer I was interested in coming in on the deal?"

"Yes. He wants to keep things as they are." She gave him an apologetic smile. "I'm sorry, Evan."

He raised his hands, then dropped them back in his lap. "I was only trying to help. It's a shame Dwyer didn't see it that way." He leaned forward with his elbows on his knees. "You don't think there's a hidden reason Dwyer didn't want me to come in on the deal, do you?"

Jenny frowned. "What do you mean?"

"Has either of them asked you to invest more money? Maybe, just maybe, this Garrett fellow isn't all he's made himself out to be." He wagged his forefinger at Jenny. "There are a great many unscrupulous men in the world. Some of them wouldn't think twice about taking money from an innocent investor, even one as lovely as yourself." His eyes lit with a smile for a moment, then turned somber again.

"Be on your guard, that's all I ask. And if you hear anything that gives you the slightest reason for doubt, I want you to come to me with your concerns. Will you do that?"

Jenny's lips parted in an amused smile at his earnest words. "You mean you'll be willing to give me advice on my investment as a bonus to our business relationship?"

Evan's expression softened. He scooted his chair forward until his knees almost touched hers. Reaching for Jenny's hands, he clasped them in his own.

"I've been meaning to talk to you about that. . .our relationship, I mean."

Jenny's fingers grew rigid in Evan's grip. More than anything, she longed to snatch them out of his grasp, but forced herself to hold still and hear him out. "What do you mean?"

Evan stroked circles on the backs of Jenny's hands with his thumbs and cleared his throat.

Jenny's fingers tensed even more, as though they would start twitching at any moment. She fought down the ridiculous impulse, wishing Evan would get on with it. Never before had he seemed at a loss for words.

"I've given it a lot of thought," he continued, his confidence seeming to return. "We make a good team, you and I.

I think it's time to make our partnership a permanent one."

"Permanent?" Jenny drew her brows together, trying to comprehend his meaning. "What could make it any more permanent than what we have now?"

Evan's mouth turned downward in a rueful grimace. "You're not exactly being flattering, my dear." He cupped her chin in one hand, keeping the other wrapped around her fingers. "What I'm saying, Jenny, is that I think we ought to get married. What do you say?"

"Married!" Jenny's whole body stiffened, and she felt her arms start to tremble. "Evan, I—"

"Don't tell me it hasn't crossed your mind," he murmured, leaning forward to brush his lips across her temple. "We're a lot alike, you and I. With your head for business and my nose for new opportunities, we could control half the money in this territory. And how lucky for me that this brilliant business mind comes wrapped in such a desirable package."

He lifted her chin and lowered his lips to hers.

"No!" Jenny yanked her left hand free and planted it in front of Evan's lips.

She drew back and tugged her right hand, but Evan didn't loosen his grip. He sat quite still, studying her with steely gray eyes, keeping her hand pinned in his grasp.

"Is this some obligatory demonstration of maidenly modesty? I can feel you trembling." A low chuckle rasped in his throat. "I think you want this kiss as much as I do."

Jenny shook her head mutely. Fragments of memories shot through her mind: other hands holding her against her will, other voices declaring their intention to have a kiss. She pulled her hand again, and this time Evan let it go free.

"Very well." He leaned back in his chair and gave her a lazy grin. "Whatever the reason, I'm willing to hold off—for a time, at least." He reached out his hand to caress her hair but drew back when she flinched. "I'll give you time to think it over, but my offer still stands, my beautiful Jenny."

Jenny stood without a word and exited through the front door, leaving it standing open behind her. *Let him lock up.* All she wanted at that moment was to escape his clinging hands and the memories they stirred.

She walked quickly along the dusty street, skirting a group of little boys playing with a ball. Her head throbbed with questions. Whatever had possessed Evan to make such an outrageous proposal? She scrubbed her hands back and forth, trying to rub away the sensation of being imprisoned within his grip.

Safely home again, she closed the door and leaned against it, pressing her fists against her temples. Had she done anything to encourage such behavior? She couldn't think of anything—word or action—that would have given Evan cause to think she'd welcome his advances.

But then, hadn't she been the recipient of unwanted advances before? And none of them her conscious doing. Did she emanate some kind of inviting signal unbeknownst to herself?

What made Evan ask that preposterous question? While receiving an offer of marriage had to rate higher than being pawed by drunken saloon patrons, she wasn't ready to give up her independence. After working so hard to achieve that goal, she wasn't about to relinquish it now.

Not to Evan, not to any man.

With a low groan, she sank to the floor and cradled her head against her knees. What was it about her that seemed to bring out men's base desires?

# thirteen

Hands. Clutching hands. Grabbing at her, plucking at her hair, her arms, her waist. Jenny tried to slap them away, thinking at first they belonged to Evan. Then Martin Lester's leering face appeared, and she realized the nightmare had returned. She struggled to waken, but the hated dream prevailed, pulling her down into its tangled depths.

Once again she relived the horror of being bundled into the burlap sack, of feeling like she was about to be shaken apart during the jolting ride in the wagon bed. Of being spilled out on the cabin floor like so much baggage. Martin Lester's drunken leer and Burleigh Ames's dark anger. . .

"What about selling her again?" No matter how many times she heard Martin Lester's suggestion, it never failed to renew a debilitating fear inside her. "Maybe down in Mexico this time. Or we could trade her to the Indians."

"Yeah." Burleigh Ames's gaze lit up with anticipation. "Yeah, that'd work." He glared at Jenny with hate-filled eyes. "But I vow I'm going to get some satisfaction first for all this grief." He wiped his mouth with the back of his hand and hitched up his belt.

"Hold on," Lester protested. "What have you got in mind?"

Ames shoved Lester to one side. "I'm not letting her go until she's paid for what she's done."

Jenny watched him make his way toward her, one slow, heavy step at a time. He grabbed her shoulder with one meaty hand and jerked her upright. "Come here," he said, his voice low and tight. "Let's see what it's like to kiss you."

Caught in his viselike grip, Jenny could only turn her head to one side. His mouth grazed her cheek.

"Hold still!" he bellowed, trying to pin her shoulders and force his lips to hers at the same time.

Jenny squirmed and pushed against his chest with all her might.

"Grab her hair and hold it tight!" Ames shouted.

Lester's fingers twined through Jenny's hair and twisted it into a tight knot. Burleigh Ames drew his lips back in a triumphant smile and leaned closer.

Jenny clamped her teeth together.

With a howl of pain, Ames flung her away from him. She flew as far as the length of Lester's arm, then jerked to a stop, caught by his hold on her hair.

Ames cursed. "Maybe I'll just kill her now and save us all a lot of trouble."

"You don't want to do that," Lester whined. "I don't intend to hang for no murder." He swung Jenny around by her hair and shoved her toward the cookstove. "Get over there," he ordered. "If you can't be of any other use, at least you can fix us some supper."

Jenny caught herself on the stove's edge. She had won. . . for the moment. But another time of testing would come. And another, and another. How long could she expect to hold out?

Once again, her heart sent up a desperate plea: "God, help me. Please, please help me!"

Jenny bolted awake, her gaze darting frantically around the dark room, straining to discern any hidden danger that might be lurking there. She pushed herself upright and scooted back against the headboard of her spool bed, wrapping her arms around her knees and listening for any telltale sounds. Only her ragged gasps broke the silence. A faint breeze wafted through the open window and she shivered, realizing for the first time that her sheet was soaked with sweat.

❧

Andrew dodged a trio of chickens pecking in the dust of Camino Real and turned down Calle del Arroyo in the direction of the Pueblo Restaurant. He strode at a steady pace, the same tenacity that helped him sift through endless assay reports in search of prime investments now standing him in good stead as he took on what might prove to be his biggest challenge yet: winning the confidence of Jenny Davis.

No matter how hard he'd tried to get in her good graces, the wall of hostility he'd sensed in her had only grown stronger.

But that was about to change. It had to. A successful partnership couldn't exist with that kind of strain between them. And he certainly couldn't entertain hopes of a budding romance if she wouldn't even give him the time of day.

He glanced at the sun overhead, an hour past its zenith. He had timed his visit to coincide with the end of the midday meal, hoping he could be her last customer of the afternoon. If only the two of them were in the restaurant, she'd have to talk to him, to tell him to leave if nothing else. At this point, almost any form of conversation would be a breakthrough.

Pushing the door open, he entered the dining room, grateful for its relative coolness after the midsummer heat outside. Manuel glanced up from serving a plate of fried chicken to another customer and favored him with a brilliant smile.

"Welcome, *Señor* Garrett," he said, hurrying to Andrew's side. "Did you come just to talk to *Señorita* Davis, or do you want to eat also?"

"I could use a good meal." Andrew smiled, heartened by the boy's contagious exuberance. "What's on the menu?"

"Fried chicken, roast beef, and pork chops. All cooked by my mother. All very good. What would you like?"

Andrew made a show of giving the list serious consideration. "I believe I'll try the roast beef."

*"Bueno.* That is a good choice."

"You recommend it, do you?"

"It is all we have left." Manuel flashed him an impish grin. "You are our last lunch customer."

Andrew chuckled at the boy's saucy rejoinder and settled himself in a chair while Manuel hustled off to the kitchen. He glanced around the dining room. No sign of Jenny, but he knew she would be somewhere on the premises, most likely in her office. And it looked like his timing had been right on target. Only three other diners remained. It wouldn't take much effort to linger over his meal and make sure he was the last one to finish.

Manuel served the roast beef with a flourish. Andrew smiled his thanks and bowed his head before concentrating on his food, one slow bite at a time.

One by one, the other diners left, until Andrew alone remained. Manuel darted back into the room to wipe the table left by the last vacating customer. "You are almost finished, *Señor* Garrett? Yours are the only dishes left to wash before we close the restaurant."

Andrew mumbled an apology and hurried through the last few bites of roast, berating himself for keeping Manuel and his mother from finishing their work.

He laid his napkin next to his plate, then stood, hesitating. He'd been so certain he could catch Jenny if he only stayed around long enough, but apparently it was not to be. He straightened his jacket and turned to leave.

Jenny opened the door to the office at that moment and the two of them stood staring at each other. Andrew saw her start to turn, then check herself, as though her first instinct had been to whirl around and slam the office door in his face. With her wide eyes and parted lips, she looked like a startled doe poised for flight. Then she pulled herself erect and the aloof mask dropped over her face.

"Did you want something?" The quaver in her voice didn't match the coolness of those aquamarine eyes. Her obvious uncertainty tugged at Andrew's heart.

"I just finished eating. A wonderful meal, I might add." He dropped his plan of compelling her to talk to him, during this visit at least. How could he force a confrontation and still call himself a gentleman?

He took a step toward the door and saw her shoulders sag in relief. Obviously, he'd made the right decision. A skittish quarry like Jenny wouldn't be won over by heavy-handed methods.

Quarry? The thought stung his conscience. This woman was not a prey to be stalked and hunted as a trophy. That kind of thinking belonged to a mentality that saw women only as objects of pleasure, a mentality Andrew abhorred. But the fact remained that the more Jenny pulled away, the more he felt drawn to her.

He had gleaned a few personal details about Jenny from Red. The old miner had been sparing in his comments, but said enough to let Andrew know Jenny was without a family. Andrew knew she had recently relocated to Tucson from Prescott. If she had no family, she must have come there on her own.

Or with Evan Townsend. From Red, he had learned of Evan's half interest in the Pueblo Restaurant. Could Evan and Jenny be more than just business partners? That might explain her coolness toward him. A sick feeling twisted in his stomach at the idea, but he put that thought away. Whatever the reasons for Jenny's reserve, he could not believe she was romantically involved with Townsend. A light of purity radiated from Jenny. She was blameless in that regard; he had no doubt of that.

And talk about courage! He couldn't imagine the kind of spunk it took for a young woman to strike out on her own like that. It showed a strength of character he deeply admired. The kind of character he hoped to find in a wife someday. And could Jenny Davis someday be that wife? The thought tantalized him. *I guess I'll just have to wait and see what You have in mind, Lord, won't I?*

❧

Jenny waited until the door closed behind Andrew, then moved to slide the bolt in place. She let her body sag against the wooden plank, glad for the safety it represented.

Last night's dream still lingered all too vividly in her mind, the memory of those grasping hands all too fresh. Her office had proven a welcome hideaway, its sense of sanctuary almost allowing her to forget the whole ordeal. Then she'd opened the door and come face-to-face with Andrew Garrett.

Had her face betrayed her anxiety at seeing him? She knew in her heart he wasn't of the same stripe as Martin Lester or Burleigh Ames, but something about his commanding presence and steady gaze made her feel vulnerable, as though he could see straight into her heart.

A knock vibrated the wood under her shoulders. Jenny jumped back, her hands pressed against her cheeks, then forced herself to relax, laughing at her foolishness. The last time this happened, it had only been Red on the other side of the door.

She debated a moment, then squared her shoulders and slid the bolt back. She would not let her bad dreams get the best of her. They filled her with horror enough during the night hours, and she could do little about the effects that lingered on into the day. But if she allowed them to control her whole life, then Lester and Ames had won after all.

Determined to conquer her fears, she swung the door wide with her head held high.

A stranger stood on the other side of the threshold, and Jenny's brave resolve melted away like a skiff of late spring snow.

"You don't remember me?" the stranger asked.

Jenny blinked, sensing a spark of recognition but unable to place the man.

"I need to leave this with you." He held out an envelope. "Would you please see that Townsend gets it?"

Jenny's memory clicked into place the moment her fingers touched the envelope. "Of course!" She looked up at the hatchet-faced man with a smile. "You left a message for him once before."

"You do remember me, then." His eyes held a glint of triumph. "I would hate to think I'd failed to make any impression at all on such a pretty lady."

He stepped back with a half bow, and Jenny closed the door on both him and his obnoxious flattery. She fingered the envelope curiously. It wasn't thick enough to hold a pile of greenbacks. At least it wasn't someone coming to deliver some of Evan's gambling winnings, she thought grimly.

She twisted the envelope gently. No, it was much too thin to hold any substantial amount of cash. It didn't feel like it contained more than a single sheet of paper.

Why would that man continue to deliver messages to Evan at the Pueblo when he looked like he would be more at home among some of Evan's saloon cronies? She shrugged. The envelope and its strange bearer were Evan's business, not hers. She had enough to think about between the restaurant, learning about her mine investment, and trying to figure out how she felt about Andrew.

Without a sound to announce his presence, Evan stepped through the office doorway. Jenny shrieked and lurched back against the front door.

"Jumpy today, aren't you?" Evan asked, his gray eyes glowing with suppressed mirth.

Jenny tried to laugh and smoothed her hair back with shaking hands. *What's going on today? Every time I turn around, someone's popping up unexpectedly.* "I'm just getting ready to leave," she said. "I had a couple of customers stay later than usual."

"My good fortune." Evan moved nearer to her and slouched against the wall, a pleased smile warming his chiseled features. "I was hoping I'd get to talk to you. . .alone."

A prickle of unease ran up Jenny's arms. Hadn't he caused her enough distress already with his audacious proposal and the nightmare it set off? The dream had haunted her throughout the day, making it impossible to concentrate or accomplish anything worthwhile.

Why, she'd barely been civil to Andrew. What must he have thought when she stared at him in the same way she'd look at a toad in her bedroom? Hardly the way to cement a solid business relationship.

She remembered the envelope in her hand. "I'm glad you stopped by," she said. "I needed to give you this. That same man dropped it off for you just a few moments ago." She held the envelope out to him, hoping the change of subject would divert his attention.

Evan straightened and moved nearer, so close the scent of bay rum tingled her nostrils. He took the envelope and tossed it negligently on the nearest table, then planted his hands against the door, one on either side of her.

Jenny drew back, pressing her shoulder blades against the unyielding door. Her heart raced and her legs quivered so, she feared they would refuse to hold her up.

Outwardly, she tried to maintain a semblance of calm. Not for anything did she want Evan to know how his approach chilled her. She lifted her chin and stared into his eyes. Eyes the color of a cloudy day, with a gleam that had surely set many a young woman's heart aflutter. Why didn't they have that effect on her? Granted, her heart was pounding at an alarming rate, but it was a speed born of near panic rather than infatuation.

Holding her arms rigid, she fought down the urge to shove him away and make her escape out the back door. If she ran now, he would always have the upper hand.

"What did you want to see me about?" she asked, pleased at the cool note she injected into her voice.

"Do I have to want to see you about anything specific, Jenny?" He trailed the fingers of his right hand along her cheek, then cupped her shoulder. "Maybe I just wanted to enjoy your presence, nothing more."

She forced a smile to her lips. "Well, you've seen me. But it's been a long day, and I didn't sleep very well last night. If you'll excuse me, I need to be getting home. It's siesta time, you know."

A look of irritation flashed across Evan's face, to be replaced by a regretful smile. Rather than stepping back to release her, he bent his head nearer to hers. "Ah, Jenny. You do have a way of keeping a man humble, don't you?"

Without warning, he pulled her into his arms and crushed his lips against hers. Jenny struggled to push him away, but he wrapped his left arm around her, clamping her arms tight against her sides.

Panic seized her, and she acted purely on instinct rather than thought. Twisting from side to side, she attempted to evade the unwanted embrace. In response, Evan moved forward, pinning her between himself and the door.

A dark fog swirled through Jenny's mind, threatening to engulf her. Just when she thought it would overtake her entirely, Evan released his hold and stepped back, a satisfied grin creasing his face.

"I know I promised you time to think things over, but I wanted to give you a convincing reason to say yes."

Jenny stared at him, her chest heaving, her whole body shaking so hard she could barely stand. "And you think that speaks in your favor?"

He threw back his head and laughed. "Don't tell me you didn't enjoy it. Why can't we be honest with each other? For whatever reason, you're determined to hold on to this pose of outraged virtue, but you don't have to keep up that pretense with me. I've known too many other women to believe in that for a moment." He lowered his voice to a low purr. "Go ahead, Jenny. Why not give in to your feelings?"

*You have no idea what I'm feeling right now.* Before she could stop herself, Jenny's hand flashed out and struck Evan full on the cheek. He fingered the bright red imprint her fingers had left, his eyes clouded with a look of disbelief.

Jenny folded her arms across her chest in an effort to stop their trembling and drew herself erect. "Don't do that again. Ever. Do you understand me, Evan? I don't need more time to think about your proposal; I can give you my answer right now, and it's no. I came here to be your business partner, nothing more, and I have no intention of changing that."

She fumbled for the bolt behind her and pulled it back, keeping her eyes on Evan all the while. "I'm going home now. I think it's best if we try to forget what just happened and keep things as they were. You tend to your other businesses and I'll run the restaurant. I'll keep you informed about anything you need to know, but the less we have to see each other, the better."

Evan only stared at her, his eyes taking on the hue of dark thunderclouds. More shaken than she wanted to admit, Jenny let herself out of the restaurant and hurried home.

She bolted her door behind her and managed to cross the room to the sofa before her tottery legs gave out. Sinking back against the cushion, she dug her fingers into the upholstery and looked around at the room she had decorated with such care. Where was the security she once felt within these walls?

Gone, she realized. Dissipated like a puff of smoke after Evan's advances. She trembled again, but this time in anger instead of fear. Back in Prescott, he had offered her a business opportunity and a new life, a chance at a new beginning. How dare he ruin it with his disgusting overtures?

Jenny dropped her forehead onto her knees, her anger giving way to despair. Had she traveled all this distance to escape her past only to find herself enmeshed in the same kind of vile trap. . .with no one to come to her rescue this time?

## fourteen

Bright sun streamed through the bedroom window. Jenny turned her head to escape its glare, and she wrapped her fingers around the bedpost, wishing she could squeeze it hard enough to chase away the pounding in her head.

Lack of sleep and the memory of Evan's behavior the day before had combined to give her the headache of a lifetime. Telling herself that morning would bring a diminishing of the pain, she had endured the incessant throbbing throughout the night hours, only to find no relief when dawn finally arrived.

Instead, she found herself unable even to get out of bed and stand. For the first time she could remember, Jenny stayed home instead of going to work. Manuel had rapped on her door, then her bedroom window, about seven, calling to her in a worried voice. After being reassured she was not on death's doorstep, he agreed to return to the Pueblo, giving Jenny his word that he and his mother could handle everything for the rest of the morning.

After he left, Jenny slipped into a restless doze and a light sleep. When she awoke, the pain seemed to have eased somewhat. Her stomach growled, and she knew she needed to get some food before hunger created its own problems.

Gingerly, she swung her legs over the side of the bed and eased herself into a sitting position. So far, so good. The throbbing quickened with the increased rhythm of her heartbeat, but it soon settled down to a dull pounding. Holding one hand to her forehead, Jenny slid off the mattress.

With faltering steps, she made her way to her tiny kitchen and sliced off a chunk of cheese. The combination of food and movement seemed to work. She felt her headache loosen its grip with every passing moment.

She risked a glance out the window, shielding her eyes with her hands as she did so. Too late now to do much good down at the restaurant. Manuel and Jacinta would be shutting down for the afternoon before she could get dressed and make her way there.

Jenny caught sight of the papers stacked on top of her cylinder-front desk. Her pulse quickened, and this time her headache didn't follow suit.

Retrieving her robe from its hook behind her bedroom door, she slipped it on over her nightgown and slid into her desk chair. She'd spent so much time on the restaurant's books, she had neglected keeping up with her own finances of late. She might as well catch up on those and feel she hadn't completely wasted the day.

An hour later, Jenny's headache had dissipated completely, replaced by excitement and a sense of wonder. She stared at the column of figures on her paper and tallied them up again for the third time.

She came up with the same total she'd gotten twice already. Could it be possible? She knew the restaurant had been bringing in a steady profit, but she hadn't bothered to tote up her own accounts for some time. When she left Prescott to start her new life in Tucson, she'd dared to dream that eventually she might earn enough to make a comfortable life for herself, but the figure that stared back at her surpassed her fondest hopes.

And that reflected the result of only a couple of months in business. If the restaurant continued to do that well throughout the coming year. . . Jenny pulled out a fresh sheet of paper and covered it with new figures, projecting what might lie ahead.

Her heart pounded and she caught her lower lip between her teeth. If business at the Pueblo did no more than keep pace with what it had done since it opened, she would be in a very comfortable position in another few months. The income from the expansion of the restaurant would only add to it.

And if the Silver Crown lived up to even a fraction of Red's expectations. . .

Jenny sank back into her chair, overcome. Without her even being aware of it, she had somehow become a woman of modest means and had every reason to anticipate her income growing even more.

She closed her eyes and let herself dare to dream of the possibilities that would open up. With that kind of income, she could build a bigger house, if she chose.

No, she decided, looking around her cozy little adobe, that wouldn't be necessary. This was her home, and a home was what she wanted, not a showplace. She might, however, add another room or two and pick up a few more pieces of quality furniture.

So what would she do with her money? It seemed ridiculous to work so hard to amass such a sum but have no idea how to use it. Some of it should be saved, she supposed. She wouldn't stay young and strong forever. But did she need to hoard all her money for a time that lay in the distant future?

Jenny left her desk and paced the room. New clothes were probably in order, but what after that? She halted abruptly in the center of the room when a bold idea shot into her consciousness.

Could she do it? Why not? She stood still a few moments longer, assessing the possibilities, then gave a decisive nod. Hurrying to her bedroom, she donned her favorite dotted-Swiss dress and dressed her hair, exulting in the fact that her headache had completely disappeared. She checked her appearance in the mirror glass one last time, then snatched up her reticule and headed out the front door. The only questions now were whether she would find Evan at the restaurant, and whether he would go along with her newly hatched plan.

☙

"You want to what?" For once, Evan was shaken out of his typically unruffled calm.

Jenny tightened her grip on her reticule. "I want to buy your share of the Pueblo," she repeated. "It's a good investment for me, and it will give you the capital you need to finance whatever business venture you sniff out next."

Evan wagged his head slowly from side to side, his gaze sweeping the dining room. "What brought this about? I thought things were—" He broke off in midsentence, and a look of understanding dawned in his eyes.

"This is about yesterday, isn't it? It's your way of putting me in my place, am I right?"

"This is a separate issue." Jenny spoke in clipped tones. "I'm a businesswoman, remember? I see this as a sound opportunity, one that will benefit us both." She held her voice steady, hoping he wouldn't guess how much she hoped he would agree to her plan. Not only would buying Evan out give her sole ownership of the Pueblo, it would also mean he would no longer have any right to come and go as he pleased. Never again would she have to wonder when he would appear next— and whether he would try to accost her. She watched his eyes, trying to gauge his reaction.

He tilted his head and gave her a long, considering look. "What if I promise to stop badgering you?" he asked. "We'll go back to the way things were originally and try to forget there was ever any unpleasantness between us. What do you say?"

Forget? Did he really imagine she could put the kiss he forced upon her out of her mind like nothing had ever happened? "I don't think you understand, Evan—"

"No, it's you who doesn't understand." His eyes narrowed and took on a steely light she hadn't seen in them before. "You want things on a strictly business basis? All right, here it is: You've made your offer; I decline to accept it."

A sense of foreboding trickled down Jenny's spine. "But why?"

"Let's just say I don't like to be thwarted. You've already made it plain that you find my attention distasteful. Now you want to be rid of my company altogether. That's hardly flattering, my dear."

Jenny felt her face flush. "I didn't say—"

"You didn't have to. That light in your eyes when you broached the idea made it plain enough. You can't wait to be rid of me. Well, I'm not going to make it that easy for you." His lips parted in a slow, cruel smile. "You're stuck with me, Jenny. Stuck good and proper. You can't buy me out unless I agree to it, and I don't. Is that clear enough?"

Jenny forced her stiff lips to frame an answer. "Perfectly."

Evan clenched his fist, then flexed his fingers. "We're partners, Jenny, in business if in no other way." He held up his hand as if to stave off her protest. "I told you I'd leave off pressuring you, and I'll abide by that. For now anyway." The corner of his mouth tilted up in a pale imitation of his usual easy grin. "Believe it or not, I can be a man of honor. I'm just wondering whether you demand the same hands-off policy from your other business partners."

Once again, Jenny's hand flashed toward him.

Evan caught her wrist before her hand made contact with his cheek. He pushed her hand aside and stepped back out of her reach. "Oh-ho, so that's the way the wind blows, is it? I wouldn't have thought it of you."

Jenny floundered, trying to follow this turn in the conversation. "What are you talking about?"

Evan moved away from the wall and stood before her, his hands on his hips, head tilted to one side. "It's him, isn't it? That Garrett fellow."

He stared at her like a scientist inspecting some strange new species, then gave a decisive nod. "That explains it, then. There had to be some reason you didn't want to have anything to do with me. I've known too many other women to seriously think there's any deficiency in my charm," he added with a lopsided grin, "but I'll admit you shook my self-confidence."

A more somber expression spread across his face. "Just how far has this thing with Garrett gone?"

Jenny bristled. "There is nothing between me and Andrew Garrett—or anyone else. He's a partner, that's all, just like you and I are. No less and certainly nothing more."

Evan regarded her with a quizzical expression. "Your lips say one thing, but your eyes tell me something else." He reached out his hand as if to touch her cheek but drew back when she flinched. "Not to worry, my dear. I won't trespass beyond the boundaries you've set. But don't expect me not to wonder what Garrett's great attraction is. You've dealt a blow to my masculine pride, you know."

He straightened his jacket and brushed down his sleeves. "Just remember, when you decide you've made a mistake, you can come cry on my shoulder. If I'd had any notion before of selling you my share of the business, it's gone now. I wouldn't miss this for the world."

Despite her mounting anger, Jenny couldn't help asking, "Miss what?"

Evan smirked. "Seeing the look on your face when you find out your hero isn't all you thought he'd be and you realize that I'm your best hope for happiness after all." He caught sight of Jenny's look of scorn, and a low chuckle rumbled through his chest. "Is it that frightening a thought? Just wait until you find out what kind of man Andrew Garrett really is. I'll look positively angelic in comparison." He reached for the door handle.

Loathing her weakness, Jenny caught at his arm. "Wait a minute, Evan. What do you mean, what kind of man Andrew really is? What do you know about him?"

Evan turned slowly. "Nothing. Not directly, anyway. Just some talk I've heard around town. Surely you've heard some of the whispers."

Jenny shook her head. "What whispers?" She could barely choke out the words.

"All right." Evan lifted his hands in surrender. "I didn't want to say anything until I was sure, but I guess you deserve to know. After you told me you didn't really know anything about Garrett, I made it my business to do some checking up on him." A sad smile twisted his lips. "Despite what you think of me, I do have your best interests at heart."

A cold knot formed in Jenny's chest. "And what have you learned?"

Evan shook his head sorrowfully. "I've turned up some distressing things. It seems your Mr. Garrett is involved in a number of shady activities."

The knot grew tighter. "Such as?"

A long sigh whistled from Evan's lips. "Since he came to town, a lot of mining stock has been traded. There's nothing wrong with that in itself," he hastened to add, "but unfortunately, these mines only exist on paper."

"Andrew is selling phony mining stock? I don't believe it." Even as she spoke the words, a riot of thoughts whirled through Jenny's mind. Andrew was a mining engineer, an expert in his field. That put him in a perfect position to do exactly what Evan suggested. The knot of dread became a wave of cold fury. She'd seen the same thing happen back in Prescott and knew the havoc it could wreak.

Evan broke into her thoughts. "There's more."

Jenny's shoulders sagged. What more could there be?

"I'm afraid his name has been linked to a couple of incidences of claim jumping, too. I have no proof, of course. Not yet, anyway." He strode over to her and clasped her hands lightly in his. "I'm sorry to lay this burden on you, but I thought you ought to know the kind of man you're dealing with before it's too late."

Jenny pulled her hands away, not interested in the kind of comfort Evan offered. "They're rumors," she said. "Unsubstantiated rumors."

"True enough. And I hope they turn out to be false, for

your sake." He turned toward the door. "But talk like this seldom begins without reason, or so I've always found."

He swung the door open. "Just remember, Jenny, I'll be here if you discover your shining knight is really quite tarnished after all."

# fifteen

*Worthless mining stock. Claim jumping.* Jenny stared at the closed door long after Evan left, his allegations echoing in her mind.

Could Andrew truly be involved in such activities? She went back over the times they had been together, trying to measure the man she knew against Evan's intimations. What she knew about Andrew was precious little, she realized. Only what Red had told her and the few impressions she had gleaned on her own.

And that overheard conversation in Prescott, when Andrew refused to cheat a miner he'd only met once and would probably never see again. Did that line up with a man who would defraud investors or steal another man's claim?

Jenny shook her head slowly, trying to picture Andrew taking part in anything like that and finding it impossible to do so. Where had those stories come from? Granted, Evan himself had classified them as rumors, but they had carried enough weight to linger in his memory.

What if the stories proved to be true? What if both she and Red had been duped? The partnership could be dissolved, she supposed, and she and Red could go back to the way they'd been before Andrew became a part of their lives. Nothing significant would have changed.

*Nothing? You're a liar, Jenny Davis.* Jenny clenched her fists and felt the dampness on her palms. *This is what comes of letting your guard down, of thinking for even one moment that you could allow yourself to trust.*

She pivoted on her heel and strode purposefully toward the kitchen. Too late to think about an afternoon siesta now. She might as well make some good use of her time. Paring vegetables or rolling out piecrusts, perhaps. Something to make it up to Jacinta for having missed work that morning.

Try as she might, she couldn't keep visions of Andrew's face and warm smile out of her thoughts while she worked. Why couldn't she get him out of her mind? Why had he claimed a place in her heart ever since she first heard his voice in Prescott? Without her being aware of when it happened, Andrew had become a part of the fabric of her being. She couldn't imagine the hurt it would cause if he were torn out of her life.

Which was exactly what would happen if the real Andrew turned out to be the man Evan described, and not the man of her daydreams.

Jenny scooped the curled potato peelings into a heap and put them in the trash. She should have known better. She *had* known better; she'd just chosen not to remember. And look where that lapse had gotten her.

*All right, then.* Jenny squared her shoulders. From here on out, the walls around her heart would go back up, as strong as the adobe walls that had encircled Tucson. Everything—from Evan's unwanted advances to the possibility of Andrew's duplicity—only went to prove that, barring a few exceptions like Michael and Red, men were men and simply couldn't be trusted. The sooner she convinced her heart of that, the safer she would be.

❧

"I got your message." Red stood in Jenny's doorway, a worried expression on his face. "Is anything wrong?"

Jenny led him to a bench on the east side of her house where they could take advantage of the late evening shade it afforded. She sat on one end of the bench and twisted her hands together. "I think we should take a second look at Andrew."

Red gave her a shrewd glance. "What's happened, Lass? Why this sudden concern?"

"It isn't so sudden, but I've reason to think my doubts may

have been justified." She repeated what Evan had told her. "I've never been entirely comfortable with the way Andrew came into the picture. You were the one who persuaded me he was trustworthy, remember?" She clapped her hand over her mouth. "I'm sorry! I didn't mean that the way it sounded."

The wiry miner chuckled. "No offense taken. I know what you meant." His expression sobered. "But I think your Mr. Townsend has gotten his facts wrong. I haven't known Andrew long, and that's the truth. But he and I have spent a good many hours talking. The Bible says that out of the heart come the words a man speaks. From everything I've heard Andrew say, I have to believe his heart is right before God. I'll stand by him until that's proven otherwise."

"I'd like to believe that, Red. I really would."

"Then keep on trusting, won't you? You haven't done so badly by taking this old prospector on faith, have you now?"

Jenny gave a shaky laugh. "I can't argue with you there. You've been a wonderful friend, and I have to admit you knew exactly what you were talking about when you said you'd found something that would make us secure for the rest of our lives."

For the second time, Red's smile dimmed. "For someone who's so cautious about putting their confidence in other people, you're awfully quick to stake your hopes on what that mine may bring."

Stung by his words, Jenny retorted, "It seems to me you've been awfully happy at the prospect of living the rest of your life in ease."

"Excited by the discovery, yes. But happy? All the silver mines in the world won't bring you happiness, you know. That has to come from within."

"What are you talking about? I'm happier now than I've been in a long time."

"Are you, now?" Red's keen eyes studied her. "I've seen you smile when the mood strikes you and even laugh on occasion.

But I'd be lying if I said I've ever once seen you glow with a soul-deep happiness from within."

Jenny shifted on the bench and tilted her chin. "I'm doing just fine, thank you. I have a prosperous business and a home of my own." She reached out to touch Red's arm and a small smile curved her lips. "And I have you as a friend. What more could I want?"

"Peace." Red let the word hang between them a moment before he continued. "And I'm not talking about the contentment you feel when everything seems to be going your way. I mean a peace that stays with you even when it looks like your whole world is going to fall apart." He leaned toward her. "The peace that comes from having God in your life."

He settled back against the adobe wall and fixed her with a rueful smile. "I can see by the look on your face that I've overstepped the boundary again. Don't worry. I won't be preaching at you." He planted his hands on his knees and pushed himself to his feet. "But if you ever decide you want to talk about it, I'll be pleased to tell you more. And if I don't happen to be around, take the matter up with God Himself. He's always ready to add another beloved child to His family."

Jenny stayed on the bench long after the shadows lengthened and the sun dipped below the horizon. She—as a part of God's family? Red didn't know what an impossible thing that would be.

æ

Jenny massaged her temples with her fingertips and tried to focus on the papers on her office desk. If she didn't work faster, she'd never have that order finished before fatigue overtook her. With Manuel and Jacinta already on their way home, the task should have been completed quickly in the quiet of the empty restaurant, but she couldn't seem to concentrate.

She pressed the heel of her left hand against her forehead and winced. The headache she had successfully fought off the day before threatened to return, its persistent throb increasing with every beat of her heart. The pain had disappeared shortly after she conceived the plan to buy out Evan's share of the business, she remembered crossly. If only he had acquiesced, surely the ache would have stayed away. It hadn't threatened again until after his refusal.

And her conversation with Red. Even now, his insistence that she needed God to be truly happy stirred feelings she thought she had buried long before. She pushed them to the back of her mind. She would deal with them later, if she decided to address the issue at all. Between Evan's contrariness, Red's tenacious prodding, and her doubts about Andrew's integrity, her mind already felt pulled in too many different directions.

*Skrrr.* Jenny sat bolt upright, recognizing the scrape of the back door opening, then the click of the latch. Who could be coming in at this hour? And what could they possibly want? Without making a sound, she rose from the desk and glanced frantically around the office, desperate to find something she could use to protect herself. A silver-streaked chunk of quartz, a gift Red brought from the Silver Crown, lay on a shelf. She snatched it up and held it tight, her arm cocked to swing at a moment's notice.

Scarcely daring to breathe, she slipped through the doorway into the dining room and threaded her way through the tables and chairs toward the kitchen. At the kitchen door, she paused, wondering if she should have simply made an escape through the office door. Too late now. Heavy footsteps approached the door from the other side. Jenny drew back her hand, ready to strike.

The door swung wide and she gasped. "Evan!" Her fingers went limp and the chunk of ore dropped to the floor with a *thump.*

"What's this?" Evan's eyes widened in surprise, then crinkled at the corners. "Did you think I was a burglar?" He laughed and shook his head. "Poor Jenny!" Glancing down at the fist-sized rock, he scooped it up and hefted it in his palm, a more sober expression crossing his face. "Poor *me* if I'd really been a burglar. That would have packed quite a wallop." He started to hand it back to Jenny, then set it on a nearby table instead. "Remind me not to rile you," he said with a grin.

Jenny's knees buckled, and she dropped into a chair, propping her head up with one hand. "Don't rile me." She gave Evan a shaky smile in return. "What are you doing here so late?"

"I might ask you the same thing," he retorted, perching on the edge of the table behind him. "You stayed home yesterday because you didn't feel well, and today I find you down here slaving away into the evening hours. Your devotion to duty is admirable, but please don't work yourself into an early grave."

Jenny covered her mouth to hide a yawn. "I just wanted to catch up on the work I missed doing yesterday. I need to finish putting together the order for next week's supplies."

"Then I've come at an opportune time for us both." Evan pulled a slip of paper from his shirt pocket and tossed it on the table in front of her. "I'm heading out early in the morning, so I thought I'd leave this on your desk tonight. I never intended to frighten you like that," he added.

Jenny pulled the paper closer and studied Evan's scribbled notation. "What is this?"

"A rancher who's trying to develop a new market for his beef will sell to us at a discount. If we agree to buy all our beef from him, he's willing to give us a price well below anything else we can get locally. He'll be staying at Hodges House until tomorrow afternoon."

"Wonderful!" Jenny felt her headache recede. "I'll contact him first thing in the morning." Remembering the other part of Evan's comment, she asked, "Where are you off to this time?"

"Yuma first, then up the river to Ehrenberg. I'll be back in a couple of weeks."

"I'll expect you when I see you," Jenny said, feeling more lighthearted than she had in days at the prospect of Evan's prolonged absence.

❧

Andrew looked up into the flickering light of the oil lamp and pinched the bridge of his nose between his thumb and fingers. He remembered lighting the lamp when the shadows had started creeping across the pages he was working on but hadn't noticed when the sun set completely. He snapped open the cover of his pocket watch and whistled when he saw the time. No wonder his eyes felt like they had grains of sand embedded under their lids.

He stood and stretched his arms wide, then rolled his neck from side to side. Working into the night hours hadn't been his plan, but the results were well worth it. He braced his hands on the desk and leaned over the papers there, studying his outline one more time.

As far as he could see, the schedule he'd drawn up for developing the mine was a good one. From everything he'd seen so far, the Silver Crown had all the makings of a big strike. Until the problems with the Apaches were resolved, work couldn't begin in earnest. But once they'd crossed that barrier, Andrew suspected a fortune could be in store for him and both his partners.

He thought about the Silver Crown's other owners while he carried the lamp to his bedroom and set it on the bedside table. He'd felt an immediate connection with Red the first time he'd met the feisty Irishman. Maybe it was due to the prospector's unfailing sunny attitude. More likely, it had to do with their bond as followers of Christ. At any rate, he hoped things worked out so they could get started on the mine soon. It would be grand to know that Red would be able to see his lonely years of prospecting bear fruit at last.

And then there was Jenny. Andrew pulled his shirt off and tossed it on a chair in the corner. Would knowing she would be financially secure for the rest of her days lighten her heart? He would love to do something to sweep away that terrible sadness in her eyes.

He slipped beneath his sheet and laced his fingers behind his head. What could have created such sorrow in her? What tragic circumstances could have befallen such a young woman to have left such an imprint?

He blew out the lamp, then rolled over and punched his pillow into a fluffy mound. According to Red, Jenny wasn't a believer. Had whatever left its mark on her sweet face managed to turn her heart against the things of the Lord as well? With all his heart, Andrew longed to find a way to restore her joy.

But he'd have to do that as a friend, nothing more. Jenny's lack of belief meant he couldn't take their relationship into a closer realm, much as he would like to. He closed his eyes, only to see Jenny's face. He opened them and found her image hovering in the darkness of his room. Scrubbing the vision away with the palms of his hands, he wished he knew how to handle his growing feelings for Jenny. Instead of Red's information putting a damper on his emotions, they seemed all the stronger for knowing he couldn't pursue her.

*Better pull the reins up tight before this horse runs away with you.* He pulled the pillow up around his ears and started praying for her instead, asking God to move in Jenny's life in such a way that she would see her need for Him.

# sixteen

Red burst through the office door, beaming and waving a sheaf of papers over his head. Andrew followed him inside, his gait more subdued but his smile every bit as wide as Red's. "Look at these, Jenny," Red exclaimed. "We're on our way!"

"And good morning to you, too," Jenny said, laughing. "What's gotten you in such a dither?"

"What's got me dithery? Why, it's the fine handiwork of our esteemed partner, my girl. Andrew spent all night on these plans, and just see what a grand job he's done." He bent to spread the papers out across the desk.

Jenny cast a sidelong glance at Andrew, and she watched the warm light in his eyes fade under her frosty scrutiny. Uncertainty replaced his earlier eager expression.

"Would it bother you if I run along now and let the two of you discuss this on your own?" he asked. "I need to deal with some other things I've been neglecting."

"What?" Red expostulated. "Leave us now, just when—"

"It's all right," Jenny cut in. "I'm sure Mr. Garrett has pressing business to attend to." She heard the coolness in her tone and knew Andrew had recognized it as well by the way he swung around and headed for the door.

"Thank you for all your hard work," she called after his retreating figure, hoping to salve her conscience and erase Red's look of bewilderment.

"Now, what was all that about?" Red demanded as soon as the door closed behind Andrew.

"Nothing at all. The man said he had things to do. I had no desire to keep him from them." She stepped nearer to the table, keeping her eyes focused on the papers in order to avoid Red's penetrating gaze. "Are you going to explain these to me?"

"I might," he said, folding his arms across his chest and perching on the edge of the desk. "And I might not." Jenny risked a quick peek at him through lowered lashes. He glared at her with an expression that reminded her of an exasperated schoolmarm determined to ferret information out of a misbehaving student. "I'd like to know why you sent young Andrew packing."

"I didn't," Jenny protested. "He's the one who said he had to leave." She lifted her chin and stared straight back at Red.

He shook his head sorrowfully. "Jenny lass, this has something to do with those groundless stories, doesn't it?"

"Of course not," she began, then halted and took a deep breath. "I suppose it does," she admitted. "You know I've had reservations about him from the first. The concerns Evan shared only served to reinforce them." Taking the offensive, she dared to add, "Someday you may thank me for protecting our mine."

Red snorted and slid down off the desk. "And someday I may sprout wings and fly." He stirred the stack of papers with his forefinger and fished two sheets from the pile. Scooting the other papers aside, he laid those two out for Jenny's inspection. "Let me show you briefly what your suspicious character spent all night working on. If that doesn't convince you he's on our side, I don't know what will."

Jenny's shoulders slumped. "All right, show me."

For the next hour, Red went over the details Andrew had labored over, his voice becoming more animated with every new idea he showed Jenny. After he laid the last sheet of paper atop the stack, he turned to her with a look of triumph. "We'll have to bide our time for a wee bit before the majority of the work can commence, but if this yields what Andrew and I expect it to, we'll all be in clover the rest of our days. How does that strike you, Miss Too-Suspicious-For-Your-Own-Good?"

Jenny ignored the jibe. Her heart beat wildly. She had dared to dream of the mine's success, but to see those dreams put down in black and white and by someone who knew what he was doing. . .

"It's amazing," she breathed.

" 'Tis more than that. It's an outright blessing. The Lord knew I needed something to keep me in my old age and saw fit to provide it."

Jenny ignored his reference to God's provision and allowed excitement to take hold of her in spite of herself.

"And as you see," Red went on, "it'll benefit all three of us equally. Andrew has been very careful in that regard. He thought of things neither you nor I would ever have come up with."

*Andrew again.* Jenny said good-bye to her happy day-dreams and came back to the world of reality. "Red—"

"Now, don't be getting your back up like that. Every time I mention the lad's name, you fluff up like a hissing cat."

"I'm just trying to be realistic. He seemed to appear out of nowhere." *Nowhere except my memory.* She cut that thought off sharply. "He didn't know us; we didn't know him. Think about it for a moment: Why would anyone offer to jump into a partnership with two perfect strangers for no good reason? It doesn't make sense."

"Unless you add God to the mix," Red said. "I keep telling you, Andrew is a follower of Christ, the same as me. God brings His people together as He sees fit to accomplish His purposes. When you look at it that way, it makes all the sense in the world."

"Not to me, it doesn't." Jenny sighed. "I don't mean to be obstinate, and I know beyond a doubt that your heart's in the right place. But in my experience, things just don't happen that way. I'll believe it when I see it—once the mine is in operation and I know my future is secure."

Red tilted his head to one side, making him look more like a leprechaun than ever. "But is it?"

Jenny gaped at him. "Of course it is, assuming Andrew's

assessment is even halfway accurate, and if he's the honest man you believe him to be. We'll never suffer want again as long as we live."

"Mm." Red pursed his lips and regarded her thoughtfully. "And after that?"

"After what?"

"After this life is over, how secure will your future be then?"

"After—Red, what are you talking about?"

"I think you know what I mean, Lass. None of us will live forever. All of us have to face God at some point. What then?"

Prickles of apprehension ran from Jenny's shoulders to her wrists. She slid her hands up and down her arms, trying to rub away the disquieting sensation. She attempted a laugh. "How did we get from the subject of mining to theology?"

Red took up a stance in front of the window. "The Lord Jesus told us not to put our confidence in treasures here on earth, but in the treasure we store up in heaven instead. There's nothing wrong with appreciating God's provision here, but I fear that's where your whole heart is focused. And there's more, Jenny. So much more."

"Can we just drop the subject, Red?" Jenny pressed her fingertips against her temples, wondering if another headache were coming on. "It seems to me this whole thing started when the conversation turned to Andrew, and it proves my point. Even setting aside the allegations Evan brought up, the man is a distraction. If he can set us at odds with each other even before the mine is opened, what will happen when things really get under way?"

Red scooped the papers into a pile and tapped the edges to square the stack. "Sure," he said in a tone lacking his usual enthusiasm. "We'll drop it. For now." A glimmer of humor returned to his eyes. "And I'll be agreeing that young Andrew Garrett is a distraction of the worst sort, but not for the reasons you've named. I think our Andrew has become a distraction to you in a special way—a distraction of the heart."

He sobered again. "Just be remembering what I've said. Regardless of what your high-and-mighty Mr. Townsend says about him, I'd stake my life that Andrew Garrett is a fine and honorable man." He tugged at his coat lapels and tucked the papers under his arm. "You need to give him a chance." He shut the office door quietly on his way out.

Jenny returned to her ledger entries, but the figures swam before her eyes. *Give Andrew a chance,* Red had said. She didn't dare. One fleeting encounter in Elizabeth's restaurant had impressed him so deeply on her mind, she feared she would never be able to be free of him. What chance did her heart have if she opened it up to him?

❧

Andrew stood in the sparse shade of a paloverde tree and watched Red exit the Pueblo Restaurant. The miner paused and heaved a long sigh, then walked in Andrew's direction. Andrew let out his own sigh, one of relief. He had correctly guessed the path Red would take. When his friend drew even with the paloverde, Andrew stepped out with a casual air and fell in step beside him.

They walked in silence for a few moments, then Red spoke. "And what is preying on your mind, may I ask?"

Andrew avoided the other man's gaze as they turned north along Camino Real. "What makes you think I have anything special on my mind?"

Red rubbed one hand across his jaw. "Let me see now. You left Jenny and me in a hurry, saying you had important things to do. Instead, I find you waiting outside under a pitiful excuse for shade on a blistering hot afternoon, right along the path that will take me back to my digs. And you seem to have a desire for my company. All signs of a man with a heavy weight on his shoulders, I'd say." The miner's seamed face crinkled into a broad grin. "She is a lovely lass, isn't she?"

Andrew started. "Who?" The moment the word left his lips, he knew he'd made a mistake.

Red laughed long and loud. "Oh, Andrew, my boy, it's a good thing you set your mind to be a mining engineer. You'd never make it on the stage. 'Who,' he says. Why, our Jenny, of course."

Andrew felt a flush begin at his collar and work its way upward toward his hairline. "That obvious, is it?"

"So you're admitting it freely, are you? Good lad. That saves me the trouble of prying it out of you." Red chuckled at Andrew's chagrin and clapped the younger man on the shoulder with his work-hardened hand. "Don't be looking so downhearted. I don't believe the lady has found you out, if that's what you're worried about."

"That's a good thing. It would only give her one more thing to despise me for."

Red shot him a sidelong glance. "And why should the lady despise you?"

"That's what I wanted to talk to you about," Andrew admitted. They stepped inside Solomon Warner's store, and each ordered a bottle of sarsaparilla. When the genial owner had handed over their drinks, they carried the bottles outside and resumed their walk.

"What have I done to put her off so?" Andrew asked.

Red took a long swallow of his drink. "Before we go any further with this, let me get one thing straight in my mind." He peered at Andrew soberly. "You realize, don't you, that our Jenny isn't a believer? Anyone with an eye to see can tell you have feelings for her. But there's a danger there, Lad. Don't let your heart go further than where God is leading. You don't want to become entangled in something that will only bring both of you heartache later on."

"I know." Andrew stared at the line of trees bordering the Santa Cruz River and set his jaw. "I know, and I realize it means I can only be a friend to her. But I want to do at least that much. I don't know what's happened in her life, but I have a feeling she needs all the friends she can get."

"Aye." Red took the last swig from his bottle and nodded agreement. "You're right about that."

"Then why is she so cold toward me? I've seen warmer glances from a dead fish than the one she gave me this morning." Just speaking the words made him feel the rebuff afresh. "It isn't as though I've given her any reason to dislike me. None that I know of, that is. But every time I come around, she pulls away, and I don't understand why."

Red looked off into the distance but kept silent.

"Every time I look into her eyes. . .have you noticed? Even when she's smiling, her eyes seem to hold such sorrow. She reminds me of a lost little girl."

"Aye, Lad." Red nodded slowly. "She's that, all right. Lost and alone and without a Savior."

"But why? What's happened to make her that way?" Andrew tried to catch Red's gaze, but the older man's glance skittered past his and focused on a point across the river. Andrew went on, feeling as though he was picking his way through a maze. "You know something, don't you? Something you haven't told me?"

The miner knotted his hands, then spread them out flat against his thighs and turned toward Andrew. "I can't be telling all I know. It was told to me in confidence, and I intend to keep it that way. But I'll say this much, since you've guessed some of it on your own: She does have reason to shy away from men. Good reason. And I suspect she feels special cause to be apprehensive around you."

The words hit him like a blow. "Me? What are you getting at?"

Red's posture relaxed, and he gave Andrew an impish grin at variance with his earlier solemnity. He took his time choosing his words. "Only that being able to trust comes hard to Jenny." His grin grew wider. "And she may feel she has as much reason to mistrust herself as anyone else."

Andrew felt his forehead pucker. "Meaning?"

Red shook his head. "If your aim was no better than your

thinking, you wouldn't be able to hit a hole in a ladder. Meaning, my dense young friend, that your feelings for her are not entirely unrequited. Do I need to spell it out further?"

"Are you saying. . . ?"

Red raised his arms and looked up, as if beseeching help from heaven. "It's a good thing God loves the simpleminded. The girl cares about you. Can I say it any clearer than that?"

A warm spring of hope bubbled forth inside Andrew. And that was where the danger lay, he reminded himself. He wouldn't—couldn't—let those feelings take control. "What makes you think so?" he asked cautiously.

Red let out a loud guffaw. "Being in the same room with the two of you is like standing in a field where lightning is about to strike. There's the same kind of spark, the same tingling feeling that sends my hair standing on end. Good thing I'm only a bystander. I don't think I could take the full force of it."

Joy surged through Andrew, then died away as quickly as it had come. As a follower of Christ, he couldn't link his life with that of an unbeliever. As much pain as it would cause him to deny his deeper feelings for Jenny, he would have to do just that and concentrate on being her friend, nothing more. To do otherwise would be totally unfair to both him and Jenny. "God has given me a mixed blessing. . .and a very tough assignment."

"Aye, Lad." Red gave him a look full of sympathy. "I know it won't be easy for you. But remember, we have a partnership to think of, and don't think for a moment that it came about by chance. I don't believe in chances. God had a purpose for bringing the three of us together, and I'm looking forward to finding out what it is. Maybe it's only to stand by young Jenny and show her there is still room for trust and hope in this world." His eyes took on a mischievous gleam. "Or maybe He has plans yet for an even greater partnership for the two of you someday. Whatever the case may be, I think it'll be worth watching this play unfold."

He turned the empty bottle in his hands and fixed Andrew with a piercing gaze. "Are you willing to walk this path not knowing what God has in mind in the end, even if it means friendship is all you'll ever have between you?"

*Am I?* The question made Andrew take a long look at the innermost motives of his heart. Could he stand back and offer Jenny his friendship, knowing he might never have anything more? Could his love for Jenny be refined in the fire of self-denial until it shone forth as a reflection of God's love for her? He nodded slowly, meeting Red's gaze. "I'm willing." *But I'll need Your help, Lord, and a lot of it.*

# seventeen

Manuel bustled up to the corner table where Jenny was working. "My mother wishes to know if she can leave a few minutes early and let me finish cleaning the kitchen for her. *Mi abuela*, she's sick and my mother is worried about her."

"Your. . .oh, your grandmother," Jenny said, recognizing one of the Spanish words she had picked up from her employees. "Of course, Manuel. Tell her to go, and I'll help you clean up."

"It is not necessary." He puffed out his small chest. "I am a good worker."

"A very good worker," Jenny agreed. "Now go tell your mother she can leave. And have her take some of that barley soup. It ought to be good for your grandmother." She watched Manuel scurry back to the kitchen, her thoughts returning to the dilemma posed by Evan's allegations against Andrew.

To her surprise, the doubts raised by those allegations wrestled against an unexpected desire to believe Andrew Garrett was everything he purported to be. The struggle haunted her waking moments and interrupted her sleep at night. How could she believe such outrageous claims? But how could she give Andrew the trust necessary for their partnership to succeed unless she knew for sure whether they had any factual basis?

*I have to know.* Despite Red's confident assertions, she couldn't just accept Andrew's innocence on faith. She needed proof—needed it now, before too many more sleepless nights took their toll. But how could she hope to get it?

She couldn't very well go up to Andrew and ask. Nor could she follow him and keep watch, hoping to pick up information that would prove or disprove his innocence once and for all.

She made another entry in her ledger, then laid her pen down and considered her options. What if she could find someone to act for her? Someone she could trust to investigate without letting Andrew know of her interest. She turned the idea over in her mind. The more she thought about it, the more she wanted to do it. But where could she find someone she could trust who was clever enough to pursue Andrew unnoticed?

Manuel cleared away more of the lunch dishes, slipping in between the tables with grace. Jenny stared after him, an audacious thought forming in her mind. *No.* She couldn't possibly. The idea was ridiculous. And yet. . .

He returned and started wiping off the empty tables. Jenny watched him work. Small for his age, he could easily give the appearance of a little boy interested in nothing more than childish pursuits, thereby keeping him from danger. Clever? Without a doubt. And his ability to hear conversations, whether or not they were directed at him, was legend around the Pueblo.

Would he be willing to perform such a task? She thought of his glee whenever he passed along some tidbit of information he'd overheard from one of their customers. He'd love it. Now all she had to do was convince him he had to stay safe.

After she ushered their last customer out and dropped the bar on the door in place, Jenny swept the dining room, over Manuel's protests. "Let me help," she told him, trying not to laugh at his offended scowl. "We need to finish quickly. There's something I need to talk to you about."

A gleam of curiosity replaced Manuel's frown, and he peppered her with excited questions. "Is something special going to happen? You are planning a party, perhaps? Can you tell me about it while we work?"

"No, no, and no," she replied to his entreaties. "Let's get this work done so we can talk."

With the cleanup finished in record time, she carried a cup of coffee and a glass of milk to a table and gestured for

Manuel to sit down across from her. "I have a job that needs to be done by someone I can trust," she began, scooting the milk over to his waiting hands. "Would you be interested?"

He lifted the glass to his lips and swallowed deeply before setting it down again. A milk mustache decorated his upper lip. "What kind of job?" he asked. "Something you need a strong man to do?"

Jenny took a sip of coffee to hide her amusement. The combination of masculine pride and the white streak above his mouth would be her undoing if she weren't careful. "Definitely," she told him. "I need you to get some information for me."

The boy's expression clouded. "Why do you not just ask for it yourself?"

*Why, indeed?* Jenny pondered the best way to answer and decided to be candid. "It's information about a person. Information he might not be willing to give me if I asked."

"Ah!" Manuel's eyes lit up. "It is something secret, then?"

"It could be. I'm not certain exactly what we may find." She studied the little boy's face. "Do you think you'd like to try?"

"It sounds exciting," Manuel said. "What do you want me to do?"

They had arrived at the sticky part. "Do you know Mr. Garrett?"

"Ah, *Señor* Garrett! He is the tall man, *sí*? The one whose eyes glow like candles when he looks at you?"

Jenny stared, dumbfounded. "What are you talking about?"

"And when he comes into the room, your face does this." Manuel twisted his own features into a look of unbridled rapture. "That is the one, yes?"

Jenny pressed her hands against her cheeks, feeling them grow warmer by the second. "I do no such thing!"

"Ah, but you do, *Señorita* Davis," Manuel continued, unperturbed by her agitation. "My mother has noticed it, too. She told Aunt Rosa only the other day that she would be surprised if you two were not married before the year is out." He looked at Jenny with a happy smile. "That is the man you mean, is it not?"

"No. That is, I don't. . . Yes, I suppose it is." Surely she didn't look as calf-eyed as Manuel's imitation would have her believe. "But it isn't what you think. It isn't like that at all." She straightened her shoulders in her most businesslike manner. "I need you to find out everything you can about Mr. Garrett. Follow him if you need to, but don't let him catch you at it. Or if he does, make sure he doesn't suspect what you're up to. Do you understand?"

Manuel nodded gravely. "You think he may have another sweetheart, and you wish to know for sure."

"No!" Jenny looked at Manuel in horror. "I barely know the man. I don't know whether he has a sweetheart, and I don't care one way or another. I simply need to know what he's up to. Businesswise, that is."

Manuel crinkled his forehead. "But you and he do business together, no?"

Jenny searched for a way to explain. "It is possible," she said, choosing her words with care, "that Mr. Garrett may be involved in selling stock for mines that don't exist. I don't know this for sure, you understand, but I would like very much to find out whether it is true."

"Aah." Manuel released a long, happy sigh. "You wish me to be a. . .a spy, is that the word?"

"That's the idea," Jenny agreed reluctantly. "But I don't want you to do anything that would put you in any danger. Do you understand, Manuel? I want you to be very careful, or I won't let you do this at all."

Manuel drew himself up with every indication of wounded dignity. "Of course. He will never know what I am about. I will be like the cougar that stalks its prey."

"Better be more like a little mouse that hides in a corner," Jenny replied. She felt a sudden prick of doubt about the wisdom of this course of action. "Do you think you can handle it?"

Manuel rose and placed his hand over his heart. "*Señorita* Davis, I will be the finest spy ever."

&

Andrew shielded his eyes from the glare of the afternoon sun as he wended his way back to his rented house. Once he went over the assay reports he had tucked in his coat pocket and sent in his final report, his obligation to the Denver Consolidated Mining Company would be completed. The prospect of being free to concentrate on his own interests here in Tucson—business and personal—put a spring in his step.

A lumbering freight wagon bound for Lord & Williams's warehouse rounded the corner and headed toward him. Andrew pressed against the wall of the building behind him to let it pass on the narrow street. He had just started on his way again when he heard a voice call his name from a small plaza up ahead. Andrew squinted against the sun and grimaced when he recognized the three men who hailed him with genial smiles.

"Garrett!" the tallest one called again.

Andrew sighed and crossed the road to join the three where they clustered underneath a mesquite tree. A small boy pattered up behind him and squatted in the dirt at the base of the tree. Andrew took a second look at him, recognizing Jenny's helper, Manuel. *Where did he get those ragged clothes?* Andrew wondered. He'd never seen him wear anything like that around the restaurant.

Manuel paid no heed to the men around him but scooped up a pile of mesquite beans and laid them out in an intricate pattern, apparently intent on some child's game. *Cute kid*, Andrew thought. He wished he could spend time talking to him instead of the men now grinning at him eagerly.

"Have you had a chance to look over the papers we gave you?" The tall man apparently served as the spokesman for the group. The others merely watched Andrew, awaiting his answer.

"I'm sorry, gentlemen. I'm afraid the claim you're offering just doesn't fit the criteria the Denver Consolidated has set."

All three men shook their heads in disgust, then the leader spoke. "You're making a mistake. That's a prime claim sure to make money for whoever owns it."

"Sorry," Andrew said again. "There's nothing I can do. Good day." He gave a curt nod and continued on his way. He'd gone over their papers, all right, and every instinct he possessed told him the claim was likely to be fraudulent. The assay report they'd given him didn't line up with what he saw on reports from the neighboring claims. He wasn't about to risk the group's money on something as suspect as that.

If he had his way, every seller of bogus mining stock would be run out of town on a rail. They preyed on the dreams of the gullible but only enriched themselves. Human nature being what it was, he knew there would always be both cheats and willing victims.

But he didn't have to like it.

❧

"*Señorita* Davis!"

The sharp whisper caused Jenny to look up from her comfortable seat on her sofa. She rose and crossed to the door. "Who is it?"

"It is I, Manuel. May I come in? I have news."

Excitement coursed through Jenny when she remembered the job she'd given him. "Of course!" She drew back the bolt and swung the door open wide.

Manuel looked over his shoulder, then flitted inside like a shadow of the night. He stood tall and erect before her, eyes flashing with pride. "I have found the answers you wanted."

Jenny peered up and down the street before she closed and bolted the door again. She sat down on the sofa and patted the cushion beside her. Manuel shook his head and stood ramrod straight before her, like a soldier reporting to his commander. Jenny half expected him to salute. "What have you found out?" she asked.

"I will tell you about my day," Manuel began. "I left the restaurant after we closed for the afternoon. You told me I could leave early to begin my duties," he reminded her. "I went first to the house where *Señor* Garrett lives and waited across the street. Soon, he came out and I followed him. He went into the assay office, then came back out again. I stayed behind him until he joined some other men. They talked for awhile, then *Señor* Garrett left."

"And no one noticed you?"

"They saw only a small boy playing in the dirt." He dropped his military air for a moment. "I have decided it is not so bad not to be tall. It can sometimes be a. . .a. . ."

"An advantage?"

"That is something that helps? Yes, then. An advantage. My cousin Rafael could not have done this," he said solemnly. "He is too big. And he is not as smart as I am, either. He would just stand there and look at the men and make them wonder what he wanted. But I," he said, puffing out his chest. "I crouch down into a little ball to look even smaller. And I look all the time at the ground, never at them." He beamed at his cleverness.

"That was very wise of you," Jenny told him. "What did you hear?"

"They talked for only a moment, then *Señor* Garrett left."

"And you followed, of course."

"No, *Señorita* Davis." He lifted his chin proudly. "I stayed."

Jenny's mouth fell open. "But why? You were supposed to find out what Andrew is doing."

"I was getting ready to follow him," Manuel explained. "I waited until he walked down the street, then before I could move, I heard something. Something that made me choose to stay."

"Don't drag this out, Manuel. What was it you heard?"

"Something one of the other men said. He was bragging to the rest, talking about 'unloading more of that worthless mining stock,'" he parroted.

Jenny blinked. "The other man? Not Mr. Garrett?"

Manuel nodded. "I learned many things this afternoon. There has been much selling of this mining stock you talked about. They wait for new people to arrive on the stage, then offer them a share in a mine. The newcomers do not know there is no mine, only a piece of paper. The man who bragged even said he told the people the quality of the ore had been verified by *Señor* Garrett." He wrinkled his brow. "Whatever 'verified' means."

Jenny sagged against the sofa cushion. "Then it's true. He really is involved in this."

Manuel's dark eyes gleamed and he bounced up and down on his toes, looking less like a professional spy and more like an excited little boy. "The stock is being sold, that is true. But it is not *Señor* Garrett who does this." He peered over each shoulder, then leaned toward her and lowered his voice to a dramatic whisper. "It is *Señor* Townsend."

"Evan?" Jenny's voice came out in a croak.

Manuel nodded eagerly. "*Sí.* He makes up the new papers for them to sell and tells them how much to ask for. The men I listened to call him their boss. They said it is his idea to use *Señor* Garrett's name to make people feel safe in buying." His face clouded. "Did I not do well, *Señorita* Davis? Why do you look so upset?"

"You've done a fine job, Manuel." Jenny parted her stiff lips and tried to shape them into a smile. "That information clears up a lot of things for me. I just need to decide what I'm going to do about it."

# eighteen

Jenny beckoned to Manuel from her office doorway. She waited until the boy scampered into the room, then shut the door with a quiet click. She knelt to his level and spoke in a low voice. "Do you think you could spend more time listening to those men without them knowing what you're doing?"

Her chest tightened when he gave an eager nod. If any harm befell Manuel, she'd never forgive herself. But the more she thought about what she'd heard about Evan's part in the mining stock sales, the more she wanted to know the whole story. She had to find out what was going on, and this looked like her only chance.

"Promise me you'll be careful," she ordered.

Manuel paused at the door and flashed her a happy smile. "Don't worry. I am like the little mouse, remember?"

❧

Three days later, Jenny found herself in possession of more information than she ever dreamed could be gleaned in such a short time. Manuel's keen hearing and knack for blending into the background had proven invaluable. From the overheard comments he relayed in his daily reports, she had pieced together an astonishing list of criminal doings by Evan and his associates.

Sitting at her desk, she pulled out the notes she had taken while listening to Manuel repeat what he had heard. She stared at the incriminating evidence spread before her. Manuel's discovery of Evan's involvement in the sales of bogus mining stock had given her a starting point for her investigation, thus opening a veritable Pandora's box of illegal activity. Jenny fumed, her anger at his betrayal growing by the minute.

Everything Evan had accused Andrew of doing reflected some wrongdoing he himself was engaged in.

She gripped the edge of the desk with both hands, trying to contain her fury. She had recognized Evan's desire for easy riches from the start. But she had never, not for one second, suspected him of being capable of this kind of amoral action.

Was she more upset with Evan or herself? She had called herself a hardheaded businesswoman. How foolish she had been! Anyone who could so readily fall prey to his easy lies had no right to pride herself on her acumen.

She rose and paced the room from the desk to the far wall and back again, then stopped abruptly in midstride. If Evan's character was so corrupt, could she trust any of the aspersions he had cast on Andrew?

For the first time in the dark days since she'd learned of Evan's perfidy, Jenny felt a flicker of hope. Could it be that Andrew Garrett was every bit the man of honor Red believed him to be? A man more like the hero of her imagination than she ever dreamed possible?

Manuel tapped on the door frame and poked his head inside the office. "*Señor* Townsend is coming. I saw him just now when I went to sweep outside."

Jenny stiffened. "He's here now?"

"He is talking to some other men down the street." Manuel jerked his head in the direction of Camino Real. "It may be some time before he gets here, but I thought you would want to know."

"You did the right thing," she told the boy. "Run along now and take care of the customers. I'll handle Mr. Townsend. And thank you for letting me know."

Manuel returned to his duties. Jenny stepped to the window and took a series of deep breaths. She could not afford to lose her temper now. She would need every shred of self-control at her command when she confronted Evan.

Gathering the papers on her desk into a neat stack, she

slid the collection of notes into a drawer and pulled out another sheet on which she had made an organized list of her findings.

She had just squared the paper on her desk when she heard Evan's voice out in the dining room. Drawing a long, shaky breath, she pushed back her chair and stood facing the door.

"And how is my beautiful partner today?" Evan breezed into the office and tossed his hat toward the row of pegs on the wall. The hat arched through the air and came to rest on the center peg. Evan grinned. "Perfect." He beamed at Jenny, then seemed to notice her lack of response for the first time. "Is something wrong?"

"Quite a lot, I'm afraid. Please close the door, Evan. We have some things to discuss."

"Aah," he said, complying with her request. "I have the feeling I'm in your bad graces once more. What is it this time? Have I failed to report on time again?"

Jenny clenched her teeth. "Nothing so minor as that." She made a conscious effort to relax her jaw and summoned all her courage. "Evan, I know."

His look of innocence would have done credit to an actor on the stage. "Know what?"

"Everything." Her throat tightened. "Look here." She jabbed her finger at the paper on the desk. "Sales of phony mining stock, claim jumping—the very things you accused Andrew of doing. I even have the names of some of your victims here. And what's this, Evan? Undercutting bids to sell supplies to the army?"

Evan bent over the sheet, his confident expression slipping for a moment before he turned to her again with his smile back in place. "But none of this has anything to do with the restaurant. What has you so upset?"

"Stop it! I'm tired of being treated like one of your gullible victims. I'm not a brainless ninny, to be lied to whenever you please. I'm your partner, remember? Partnership implies the need to be able to trust one another." She swept her hand toward the list of offenses. "How can you possibly expect me to trust you about anything now that I know about all this?"

Evan stepped back and appraised her with cool detachment. "Have I proven untrustworthy as far as the Pueblo is concerned? Have I embezzled funds or cheated you in any way?"

"N—no. At least not as far as I know," Jenny added.

"Haven't I let you run the business as you see fit?"

"Well, yes, but—"

He spread his hands wide apart. "Then what's the problem?"

Jenny stared in disbelief. "The problem, Evan, is that I *know* about these things. Before, I wasn't aware of what you were up to, but now I am. That changes everything. I can't continue in a partnership with someone who'll drag my reputation down along with his."

Evan leaned back against the door frame. "So what are you suggesting?"

"The same thing I suggested before. I want to buy out your share of the business."

"All right. Pay me a thousand dollars, and it's yours."

Jenny gasped. "You can't be serious."

"Oh, but I am, sweet Jenny. The question is, are you? How badly do you really want to buy me out?" His eyes held a gleam of triumph.

Hot bile stung Jenny's throat. "I'm very serious, but that price is outrageous. You know this property isn't worth more than three hundred."

Evan raised one eyebrow in mock sympathy. "Then I'm afraid you're stuck with me for the time being."

⁂

The door to Jenny's office stood open. Andrew tapped on the frame and peered inside, waiting until Jenny looked up. "Red wanted me to stop by and ask you—"

He stopped short. "Is anything wrong?"

Jenny shook her head mutely, but the smudges on her cheeks told him otherwise. Andrew took a step inside and reached out to wipe an errant tear away, then drew his hand back. She wouldn't thank him for pointing it out.

"Nothing's wrong," she said. "Nothing you can do anything about, anyway."

Feeling daring, Andrew pulled a chair up close to hers. If she asked him to leave, he would. But she hadn't, not yet anyway. "Would you like to tell me about it? Maybe it would help to talk it out with a friend, or partner to partner, if you'd rather look at it that way."

She waited so long to answer that he felt his hopes rise. Then she shook her head again, more decisively this time. "It's something to do with the restaurant. Nothing you need to concern yourself about. I need to handle this myself." Her mournful expression softened a bit. "Thank you for asking, though. I appreciate the offer."

There seemed to be no reason for him to stay any longer. He pushed himself to his feet. "All right, I'll be going now."

"Wait. What did Red want you to ask me?"

"He was wondering if we could all meet again tomorrow afternoon. Don't worry about that now, just take care of whatever is bothering you first." He replaced the chair, then paused near the desk. "I just want you to know that I'd like to be your friend. Please feel free to call on me if you ever need any help." He reached out and gave her arm a brief squeeze.

There it was again—that lightning-bolt feeling that surged between them. Andrew left the restaurant feeling unnerved. For the first time since he had arrived in Tucson, Jenny had looked at him with something other than disdain. Would he have that same feeling every time they came in contact? He didn't know, but he wouldn't mind finding out.

≈

Jenny stood at the window and watched Andrew walk away down the street. She rubbed her fingertips lightly over her arm. Did he have any idea how his touch affected her?

She walked back to the desk, sat down, and cradled her head in her arms. Was it possible to know another human being? Really know them? She had staked everything on building a new life in Tucson, basing her decision on the assumption that Evan's offer held the key to a brighter future. How could she have been so wrong?

Had she been wrong about Andrew, as well? The fragile hope that sprang up within her at the prospect that he might be the kind of man she secretly wanted him to be disturbed her. No, more than that. It frightened her.

If the flesh-and-blood Andrew proved to be as worthy of her trust as the man of her dreams, she might be tempted to drop the walls that had protected her for so long. Walls that seemed to be crumbling bit by bit ever since the probability of Andrew's innocence arose. More to the point, did she *want* to keep those barriers in place? That possibility bothered her even more.

≈

"Did you hear?" One of the Pueblo's regular customers sidled up to Jenny on his way out the door. "There's some big stir down at the sheriff's office. Seems a few of our local citizens have been busy selling stock in phony mines, and someone's complained about it. They'll have their hands full trying to sort this out. I've seen it happen before up San Francisco way."

Jenny nodded her thanks and tried to conceal her shock at the news. Not until she reached home that afternoon did she allow herself to focus on what this might mean for her.

She dropped onto her sofa and buried her face in her hands. What an ironic twist her life had taken! She had put her trust in one man and doubted another, only to find that the one she doubted had proven to have a sterling character while the one she trusted—her partner, no less—turned out to be a swindler.

And now that she knew it, what was she supposed to do about it? Being Evan's partner, her name had been linked to his since the day she arrived in Tucson. His illegal activities, if they ever came home to rest, would reflect on her as well.

Conscience demanded she dissolve their business relationship and sever her association with Evan. But how could she do that when she couldn't possibly meet the price he'd named?

She saw only one other possibility: turn the business over to Evan and return to Prescott. Elizabeth and Michael would offer her a warm welcome. She could return to her little room in the back of the Capital Restaurant & Bakery and pick up her life at that point again.

It would be like she'd never left. She would go back to waking up every morning looking forward to Elizabeth's companionship and Michael's teasing banter. To a routine she knew so well she could perform every bit of it by rote.

Back to wondering what she'd face every time she set foot out on the streets of Prescott. To bracing herself for the next round of insults.

How could she give up the self-respect she had fought so hard to win? The thought of having to admit defeat and return to the wagging tongues of Prescott was more than she could bear.

What if. . . For the first time since her confrontation with Evan, Jenny's hopes rose. The sheriff was even now investigating the mining stock fraud. When the law uncovered proof of Evan's crooked scheme, surely she would be able to acquire full ownership of the Pueblo and get her life back on track. Hope fluttered and died when another thought entered her mind. Would Evan's exposure help or hurt? Would their connection mean her reputation would once again be destroyed through no fault of her own?

*Not again. Oh, please, not again.*

She clenched her fists and sat bolt upright. That wouldn't happen. Not if she could help it. Hurrying to her cylinder-top desk, she sorted through the stack of notes she had brought with her from the restaurant. No doubt about it, they gave clear documentation of Evan's nefarious doings. She would give every scrap of knowledge she possessed to the sheriff. Doing so would put as much distance as possible between her and Evan's misdeeds and let everyone know she had no connection with any of it.

Jenny pored over her notes, fixing each point in her mind. When she felt sure she could recite every detail, she looked through her wardrobe and selected a dark blue dress with matching bolero jacket. Its demure lines projected the respectable image she wanted to portray. She reached for her reticule and checked her image one last time in the mirror on her bedroom wall.

A sharp rap summoned her to the front door. Jenny hesitated, wanting to avoid any interruption that would delay her visit to the sheriff. But it might be Red or Manuel. Or Andrew. She opened the door.

A tall, sober-faced man stood on her doorstep. He tipped his hat and gave her a brief nod. "Miss Jenny Davis?"

Jenny nodded warily. Then she saw the badge on his vest and brightened. "You're the sheriff?"

He seemed taken aback by her obvious pleasure. "That's right. Tom Randolph. I'd like to talk to you."

How had he known? Jenny put the question from her mind. It didn't matter. The important thing was that he was here and they could discuss her knowledge of Evan's activities. "I'm glad you came. I understand you're investigating the sale of fraudulent mining stock. I was just on my way to your office."

Again, Randolph seemed confused by her response. "I must say I'm surprised to find you so eager to talk to me."

Jenny gave him a puzzled look. "Surely you're interested in any information that would lead you to the culprits."

"Yes, Ma'am. But I don't usually come across this kind of cooperation from the person I'm investigating."

# nineteen

Jenny couldn't force a single sound from her throat. Surely she hadn't heard him correctly.

Randolph studied her for a long moment, then said, "Why don't we just walk on down to my office? We can carry on the rest of our conversation there."

He cupped Jenny's elbow in his hand and walked beside her along the dusty road. On the surface, she supposed, he looked like any gentleman escorting a lady down the street. But she could feel the iron in his grip and knew he acted the part of the gentleman only so long as she cooperated.

Her feet moved in step with his; her mind ran miles ahead. Once again, she was in the control of a man without being sure of his intentions. When she had been in the clutches of Martin Lester and Burleigh Ames, she'd prayed for some representative of the law to come along and save her. Now she was in the hands of the law, and who could rescue her from that?

But did she need rescuing? She swung her head slowly from side to side. It couldn't be. Whatever he'd meant by that comment about investigating her, surely she had taken it wrong.

They passed the Pueblo, where Manuel stood outside, sweeping the doorway in preparation for the evening customers. He looked up and beamed when he saw her approach, then frowned in confusion when she didn't smile back. His gaze darted between the badge on Randolph's vest and his hand on Jenny's elbow, then Manuel's mouth formed a silent O. Casting an apprehensive glance over his shoulder, he turned and ran off in the opposite direction, his bare feet kicking up puffs of dust.

ﾞ

"I've told you everything I know." Jenny stared at Randolph, seated on the other side of the sheriff's desk, and passed her hand across her forehead to push the damp bangs back off her brow. "I've given you names, dates, and places. I don't understand why you persist in thinking I'm a part of this."

Randolph stared back. Without taking his gaze off her, he leaned back in his chair and propped one booted foot on the corner of a half-open drawer. "That's just it, Ma'am. You've given me too much information, if you see what I mean."

"No, I'm afraid I don't," Jenny snapped, exhausted from the long afternoon of relentless questioning. "I've come forward like a good citizen and given you the information you need to solve this case and more besides. As I told you, I was just on my way here to see you when you showed up at my door."

"Mm-hm." Randolph's simple remark didn't carry any inflection, but Jenny could read the unbelief in his eyes. "If you'll pardon my saying so, Ma'am, I find that hard to believe."

Jenny bit back the hot reply that sprang to her lips, wishing she could shake herself awake from this living nightmare.

ﾞ

Andrew's long-legged stride ate up the ground between his rented house and the sheriff's office. When Manuel's steady pounding roused him from his afternoon nap, he'd been too groggy at first to take in the boy's frantic babbling.

"*Señorita* Davis," Manuel kept repeating, his eyes wide with panic. "The sheriff has her. She needs your help."

By the time Andrew sorted out Manuel's meaning, he was wide awake. Without taking time to do more than tuck his shirttail in and comb his fingers through his hair, he set out downtown to see what he could make of this business. Jenny, under arrest? For what? It didn't make a lick of sense, but there was no denying Manuel's sense of urgency.

He rounded the corner and made straight for the sheriff's office door. He shoved it open without knocking and marched inside.

Jenny sat ramrod straight on a chair facing the sheriff's desk, her dark dress making a marked contrast to the pallor of her face. Her eyes, wide blue-green pools of anxiety, lit up at the sight of him, but she didn't otherwise react to his entrance.

"What's going on?" he demanded, every protective fiber of his being springing to the fore.

The sheriff unfolded his long, lean body and rose from the chair behind the desk. "And you would be. . . ?"

He returned the man's steady gaze. "Andrew Garrett. I'm one of Miss Davis's partners in the Silver Crown Mine."

The lawman tilted one eyebrow upward and looked back at Jenny. "A newly expanded restaurant, the purchase of a house, and now a silver mine? Quite a bit of money at your disposal, wouldn't you say?"

"Money that I came by through my own hard work," Jenny retorted. She held her head as high as ever, but Andrew could see her shoulders trembling. Whatever was going on here, it was clear to him that she had been pushed to her limit.

"Are you finished with Miss Davis?" he asked. "If so, we have some personal business we need to discuss."

The sheriff shifted his gaze to Andrew and gave him a long, appraising look. "The two of you wouldn't be planning to head out of town anytime soon, would you?"

"Sheriff Randolph, I resent your implication." Jenny's voice held a note of defiance, even though Andrew knew she must be exhausted. "I'll be available if you have anything further to discuss with me."

"Oh, you can count on that," Randolph drawled. He narrowed his eyes and leaned over the desk. "I don't have anything solid to hold you on, only my suspicions. . .and you've given me plenty of those. I want you back in this office tomorrow morning at nine to answer some more questions, is that understood?" He straightened and rocked back on his heels. "If you're really the innocent party you claim to be, that shouldn't be a problem."

"I'll be here." Jenny's body quivered, but her voice held firm.

"So will I," Andrew said. He helped Jenny to her feet, alarmed by her fragile appearance. "I'm her partner, remember? She won't be here without me."

*What has she gotten herself into, Lord?*

❧

"Good morning," Tom Randolph greeted Jenny when she walked into his office with Andrew promptly at nine the following morning.

Jenny seated herself in the chair she had occupied the day before and gave the lawman a level glance. A night to reflect on the previous day's proceedings had given her a new perspective. Trying to see things from the sheriff's point of view, she could understand why he might look askance at anyone who possessed such detailed knowledge of criminal activity yet proclaimed her own innocence. No wonder her sudden spate of information had taken him off guard.

She'd had time now to think things through, to plan how to act rather than react. Undoubtedly he'd done some thinking about his own attitude as well. Today they could both start fresh and have the whole misunderstanding ironed out in no time.

And then there was Andrew. Just the thought of him being there sent a warm glow through Jenny. She had treated him abominably, yet he'd rushed to her aid without a second thought the moment he knew she was in trouble. His presence today meant more to her than he could possibly know. Red would have come if she'd asked him to, but Andrew had chosen to be there—insisted on it, in fact. He'd told her once he wanted to be her friend. That knowledge gave her the courage to straighten her spine and speak to Sheriff Randolph without a quaver in her voice.

"I assume that since you've had time to think things over, you no longer believe I'm guilty?"

Randolph took a seat behind his desk and regarded her a moment without answering, then leaned forward, his gaze boring intently into hers. "What do you know about rigging bids for army supplies?"

Taken aback by the sudden question, Jenny faltered. "Only what I told you yesterday, that I have reason to believe Evan Townsend has done exactly that."

"Miss Davis, do you know a man named Zeke Waterford?"

Jenny shook her head, trying to follow the abrupt change of direction. "I don't know anyone by that name."

Randolph's gaze never wavered. "He's a tall fellow, thin, with sharp features."

"I still don't—wait a minute." A picture formed in Jenny's mind. "That sounds like the man who stopped at the restaurant on two occasions. He left an envelope for Evan both times, but I never knew his name."

Randolph made a quick note of her response. "He's been arrested for his part in the bid rigging. One of my deputies caught up with him last night. He admits his involvement, but said he gave the information directly to you. He never mentioned Townsend."

"You mean that's what was in those envelopes?" Jenny asked. "Well, yes, he did hand them to me, but I gave the envelopes to Evan without opening them. I had no idea what was inside."

"What about Harvey Green?"

"The rancher? I ordered some beef from him for the restaurant. What of it?"

"You were seen passing money to him in the lobby of the Hodges House."

"I told you," Jenny said, her voice rising. "I was paying him for the beef I ordered. Beef from his ranch."

"There is no ranch." Randolph leaned his elbows on the desk and steepled his fingers. "Your connection with Green is what drew our attention to you in the first place. Green's only involvement with cattle is in rustling them and selling them off as his own. His big mistake was in trying to palm some of them off on the army by being the lowest bidder—information provided by you, Miss Davis."

Jenny clutched at the seat of her chair with both hands. If she let go for an instant, she feared she would topple off onto the floor. "It's Evan," she whispered. "I gave the envelopes to Evan. And he's the one who told me to order the beef from Harvey Green."

"So you say." Randolph's grim expression didn't alter. "Let's see what someone else has to say, shall we?" He stepped to a hallway at the back of the room and called out, "Come in, Mr. Townsend."

Evan stepped in and took up a position near the desk.

"You heard what Miss Davis had to say?" Randolph asked.

Evan nodded. "I heard it all." He turned to Jenny. "Why? If you needed money, you should have come to me. I'm sure we could have worked something out. You didn't need to go to such lengths. And I don't understand why you felt it necessary to use my name to cover up your own misdeeds." He dipped his chin and looked at her with a sorrowful gaze. "What have I ever done to you?"

Her grip on the chair loosened, and the floor rose to meet her.

❧

Andrew rushed to catch Jenny before she hit the hard plank floor. He scooped her up and cradled her in his arms. "Where can I put her?" he asked.

"Back here." Randolph led the way to an empty cell containing a cot. Seeing Andrew's glare, he protested, "This is a jail, not a hotel. It's the only place available."

Andrew growled under his breath but laid Jenny down on the thin mattress. He patted her cheeks and chafed her wrists until her eyes fluttered open.

"Andrew?" Her blue-green eyes looked at him uncomprehendingly. "Why am I. . .*where* am I?" She looked around at the surrounding bars and bolted upright, her mouth hanging open in a silent scream.

"It's all right." He gripped her shoulders and turned her to face him. "It's all right," he repeated, praying it was true. He pulled Jenny toward him, and when she didn't resist, he sat on the edge of the cot and wrapped his arms around her. "Shh. Take it easy." He stroked her hair as though comforting a child. "The sheriff wants to ask you a few more questions, but I won't let that happen until you're ready."

"The sheriff," she murmured. Then she stiffened. "Evan! He was here, wasn't he?" She pulled back and looked at Andrew for confirmation. "Where is he now?"

"He left just after you passed out," said Randolph, striding into the cell. "Said he had some other business he needed to see to." The sheriff propped his hands on his hips and looked at the two of them. "Are you ready to do some more talking?"

"I think she's had enough for one day," Andrew began.

Jenny laid her hand on his arm. "No," she said, "I want to be done with this." She struggled to her feet, and he helped her walk to the outer room, marveling at her courage. This woman couldn't be guilty of the charges Randolph kept heaping at her feet.

*Could she?* He didn't believe it, or at least he didn't want to. But the tiny seed of doubt planted by the mounting evidence and Jenny's inability to refute the claims refused to be uprooted entirely.

The one thread of hope that Andrew clung to like a lifeline was Evan's earlier denunciation. Every instinct Andrew possessed told him the man could not be trusted. If Evan said Jenny was guilty, it gave Andrew reason enough to think the opposite might well be true.

*❧*

"You're sure you're up to this?" Randolph's rumbling voice held a note of genuine concern.

"I'll be fine," Jenny replied. She took a sip of the water he brought her at Andrew's request. "What else do you want to ask me?"

Randolph tapped his fingers on his desk and considered the notes before him. "You still contend you had nothing to do with any of this—the mining stock, rigging those bids?"

"No." Jenny felt her former indignation return. "And I'm no rustler or claim jumper, either."

"Settle down, now. I didn't say you were."

"No, but your implications have been clear enough. I'm the one who provided the information you were looking for about the mining fraud, remember?"

"You see, that's just the problem." Randolph scrubbed his face with his hand. "I never said a thing to you about the mining stock. You're the one who brought that up, remember?"

"But you asked me—" Jenny stopped, remembering his earlier comments. No, he hadn't. His interest in her lay in her supposed involvement with Harvey Green. She had been the one to draw Randolph's attention to a possible connection with the sales of bogus mining stock. In her eagerness to bring Evan to justice, she had turned the eyes of the law on herself.

The door opened before she could say another word, and a portly man strutted in. He walked over to the sheriff and stuck out his hand. "Randolph? I'm the new owner of the Red Slipper Saloon. I understand you're one I need to see about paying my taxes." His gaze fell on Jenny and a delighted smile split his face.

"Well, look who's here!"

Jenny stared at him, her mind a blank. "Do I know you?"

The man's ample belly shook with his guffaws. "Know me? Why it's Adrian Vance. From Prescott, remember?" He turned back to Sheriff Randolph with a jovial chuckle. "I'll never forget this one, I can tell you that. The prettiest songbird who ever lightened the hearts of thirsty miners."

*No.* This couldn't be happening. Jenny laced her fingers together in a white-knuckled grip and fought back the waves of darkness that threatened to overwhelm her. She would not faint again. No one in Tucson knew of her days at the Nugget, save Red. She had left that life behind her. Or thought she had, until this talkative man showed up. She shot a quick glance at Andrew and saw his stunned expression.

Vance grinned at her again. "It's no wonder I didn't make much impression, with all those young bucks wanting your attention. I'd be a pretty poor choice in comparison, wouldn't I?" His chest shook with laughter again. "No matter." He sketched a wave at Randolph and walked back to the door. "I can see you're busy now, so I'll come back later. It was a pleasure meeting you, Sheriff. There's always a drink waiting for you at the Red Slipper. And you," he said, pointing a pudgy finger at Jenny. "If you're ever in need of a job, be sure to look me up."

Vance exited and a heavy silence settled over the room. After a moment, Randolph got to his feet and reached for the large ring of keys that hung near his desk. "I hate the thought of locking up a lady," he said. "But under the circumstances—"

"That's exactly the word for it." Andrew stepped forward. "Circumstantial evidence is all you have."

"But I need to be sure she's around to answer any more charges that may come up," Randolph said.

"Miss Davis has a business to run," Andrew told him, helping Jenny to her feet. "If you need to speak with her, you'll find her either at home or at the Pueblo Restaurant. If you want more assurance than that, I'll vouch for her."

The two men locked gazes, then Randolph put the key ring back on its hook. "All right," he said. "But you see that she checks in with me tomorrow."

# twenty

"I have to get back to the restaurant," Jenny said. "I need to help Jacinta and Manuel."

"You need to go home and rest," Andrew countered. He took her elbow and steered her through the streets in the direction of her home.

Jenny complied, too tired to argue. "Thank you for standing by me today," she told him.

"I said I wanted to be a friend to you, and I meant it." Andrew squeezed her elbow and gave her a warm smile, then his gaze turned sober. "Randolph isn't going to let go of this anytime soon, you know. You're going to need more than just my friendship to see you through this."

"What do you mean?" she asked, although she had an uneasy feeling she knew the answer.

"I mean Jesus," Andrew answered, confirming her suspicion. "You need Him as your Savior. We all do. But right now you also need someone to help you carry this burden, and He's the best one to do that."

"What if He doesn't want to?" The words were out before she could stop them.

Andrew halted in the middle of the street and caught her hands in his. "He does, Jenny, you can trust me on that. He loves you." He opened his mouth again as if to add more, then pressed his lips together. "Think about that while you're resting this afternoon."

Red jumped up from the bench outside her door when they approached the little adobe house. "How are you, Lass? Did that bully of a sheriff come to his senses?"

"I sent Manuel over last night to tell Red what happened,"

Andrew said in response to her questioning look.

"I'm all right, Red. A little worse for wear, perhaps, but doing well enough." She propped her hand on the doorpost, glad of its support. "I really do need to get back to the restaurant."

"Not on your life." Andrew folded his arms and set his jaw. "You're going to go inside and lie down. Red and I are going to sit out here and make sure no one comes by to bother you. And to make sure you don't get any notions about sneaking out and going to work."

She tilted her head and mustered up a weak smile. "Afraid I'll run away and leave you to face Randolph alone?"

"I have no doubt at all about you keeping your word." His gaze bored into hers with an intensity that made her knees go limp. She nodded, too shaken to resist further, and went inside. Alone in her room, she took off her dress and laid it across a chair, then stretched out on the bed. She felt her eyelids close as soon as her head touched the pillow.

When she woke, the sun had traveled far down in the western sky. Jenny lay still for a moment, wanting to savor the first moment of peace she had known that day.

Red's and Andrew's voices filtered in through the curtains of the open bedroom window. "So now you know the whole story," Red was saying. "I wouldn't have told you if that fat saloon keeper hadn't opened his mouth and given things away."

"It explains a lot," Andrew said. "No wonder she doesn't trust anyone." He paused a moment, then went on. "I talked to her about needing Jesus."

"Did you now?" Excitement was evident in Red's tone. "And what did she say?"

"She has the notion He wouldn't want to help her. And from what you've told me of all she's been through, I'm beginning to understand why. It's a wonder she believes anyone truly cares for her."

Jenny heard him heave a deep sigh. "I wish I knew people as well as I know rocks," he said. "Rocks don't lie to you."

"Don't be giving in to doubt, yourself," Red cautioned. "Keep on believing in our Jenny. She needs true friends who'll stand by her, no matter what. If she doesn't see Jesus for who He is, you'll have to show Him to her by your actions."

Jenny lay in her bed long after the sunlight paled and the two men crept away from their post for the night. She watched the shadows lengthen across her bedroom floor.

So she could now add Andrew to the list of those who thought all her problems could be solved by God. Did he think she wouldn't welcome that? Didn't any of them— Andrew or Red or Elizabeth or Michael—realize she longed for an acceptance she knew could never be hers?

She pushed herself up off the mattress and donned her nightdress. Tucson was no longer her haven, no more a sanctuary in which she could hide from the echoes of her past. Adrian Vance's coming had changed all that. Her hands trembled as she reached for her hairbrush. She could almost hear his booming voice describing her history in Prescott to Sheriff Randolph and Andrew.

Andrew. Her fingers tightened on the brush handle when she remembered his stricken look upon hearing Vance's words. Yes, he'd told her he wanted to be her friend, but wasn't the whole purpose behind that to persuade her she needed to turn to Jesus?

Her eyes welled with tears, and the brush clattered to the floor. Everything she had worked so hard to achieve threatened to crumble around her in ruins. First the restaurant, then her reputation, and now Andrew's regard.

She slipped to the floor and wrapped her arms around her knees, the ache of loneliness stabbing at her like a heavy blade. She had gained valuable experience running the Pueblo; she could duplicate that success elsewhere if she had to. And assuming the next few days didn't find her in Sheriff Randolph's custody, she could start anew in another town, one so far away that no one from Prescott or Tucson would ever find her.

Those things would cost her in time and trouble, but the pain that tore at her heart the most came from the thought of losing Andrew's friendship.

Jenny let out a low moan and hugged herself tighter, trying to alleviate her misery. She had pushed Andrew away for most of the time she'd known him. How could his loss now feel like such a blow? Whether it made sense or not, without Andrew, she felt more alone than she'd ever been.

"God, help me!" The cry burst forth before she realized she was going to utter it. The words hovered in the air, mocking her. Hadn't she cried out the same plea dozens of times before?

That didn't matter. Nothing mattered now except her knowledge that the only hope she had lay in the slim possibility that God would listen this time.

"God, I need You. I know I'm not good enough for You, but Andrew says You love me. So does Red. So does Elizabeth. If that's true, if You love me in spite of all the things that have happened and all the things I've done, won't You let me know it?"

A faint stirring fluttered in her heart, a whisper no stronger than the brush of air from a butterfly's passing. *Could it be?* Jenny gathered up her courage and whispered, "Is that You, God? Are You listening?" The flutter grew more insistent, spreading throughout her innermost being until it filled her with a flood of joy.

"You do love me! I believe it now. Thank You so much for not giving up on me."

Tears streamed down Jenny's cheeks. From the brink of ruin, she had been lifted up to a pinnacle of belief. Whatever happened in the morning, whatever new treachery Evan might devise, this certainty of God's love was now hers, and nothing could take that away.

⁂

Jenny stepped into Sheriff Randolph's office the next morning with a light step and her head held high. The sense of forgiveness that filled her soul still amazed her. She smiled at Andrew, who had accompanied her once again. He looked perplexed by her calm demeanor but smiled back.

Even the sheriff seemed startled by the change. "You look happy today, Miss Davis. Did you find out something that will prove your innocence?"

"No, Sheriff. I found peace." Randolph stared as though he thought she'd lost her mind, but Jenny didn't care. It was true. Becoming a child of God hadn't made all her problems go away as she once believed. The problems still existed. But now she had a place to take them. She looked at Andrew again and caught the hopeful look in his eyes. She appreciated Andrew's continued support more than she could ever tell him, but even if he changed his mind and left her on her own, she now had another Friend who would help her through her ordeal.

Randolph cleared his throat. "And just where did this peace come from?"

Jenny smiled. "I won a battle last night, Sheriff. Or rather, I lost a battle and wound up the winner." His look of utter confusion made her chuckle. "I've fought against God for years," she explained. "All the people I loved most told me He loved me and wanted to make me His child, but I knew they were wrong. You see, I thought I wasn't good enough for Him. And I was right! I wasn't. But the amazing thing is, He loved me anyway. I couldn't see that until last night, when I didn't have anyplace else to turn."

"I. . .see." Randolph shifted in his chair. "The investigation is still continuing. Check back with me tomorrow."

"I'll do that," Jenny assured him. "And if you need me any other time, you know where to find me."

❧

Andrew sat at a corner table in the Pueblo Restaurant and watched Jenny through the office doorway. She sat serenely at her desk, apparently unperturbed by the storm that raged around her. Did she have any idea of the way her face glowed?

Randolph might be dubious about the change in Jenny, but the joy that radiated from her convinced Andrew beyond a doubt.

Speaking of doubt—the memory of the skepticism he'd voiced to Red only the night before came back to haunt him. Hadn't he doubted her, too? If only there were some way he could make up for his lapse in faith, some way to clear Jenny's name without question.

Manuel sauntered up to the table and handed Andrew a cup of coffee. "She is going to be all right, is she not?" he asked in a worried tone.

"I think so. But if we could get some proof that would convince the sheriff she's innocent, it would sure help."

Manuel's face lit up. "You need help finding proof? I am very good at that. I helped *Señorita* Davis find the information about *Señor* Townsend."

Andrew turned his attention to the grinning boy. "You did?" A plan began to form in his mind. Maybe there was a way to help Jenny after all. "Manuel, do you think you could help me find a man?"

# twenty-one

An insistent pounding jerked Jenny from her sleep. She sat up and looked around, disoriented for a moment in the dark room. The pounding came again. Jenny jumped out of bed and pulled her robe from its hook. Belting it around her waist, she padded toward the front door.

"Who is it?" she called in a low voice.

"It's Evan. Let me in. I need to talk to you."

"Are you out of your mind? It's the middle of the night."

The pounding persisted. "I'm going to stand here and keep knocking, Jenny. If you don't open up, the whole street will know I'm out here."

Jenny waited in the dark living room a moment longer until the hammering on the door convinced her Evan had every intention of making good his threat. She fumbled for a match and lit a lamp.

"Will you be quiet?" she said. "Quit knocking. I'm going to open the door." She slid the bolt back as she spoke. Evan nearly bowled her over in his haste to enter the room.

"What is wrong with you?" she blazed at him. "Isn't it enough you've dragged my name through the mud? Now you show up at this hour—you're going to destroy what little is left of my reputation."

"I wanted to tell you I'm sorry," he said. "I couldn't stand to wait until morning to get that off my conscience."

Jenny held the lamp higher and looked at him more closely. The light showed dark circles under Evan's eyes that hadn't been there before. Could he be telling the truth for once?

"All right, you've told me. Now go away. I'm near to being

arrested, Evan. For something you've done. I'm afraid your apology won't do much to change that."

He held up one hand. "No, wait. That's why I wanted to see you tonight. To tell you I'm sorry and that I want to make it right."

Jenny eyed him narrowly and waited.

"I know I've put you through a rather bad time." Evan caught her angry gaze and flinched. "All right, a terrible time. And I am truly sorry. I'm going to talk to Randolph in the morning and tell him that you had no part in any of it. It was all my doing."

Jenny set the lamp down before she dropped it in her shock. "You'd do that for me? Why?"

"Call it an acute attack of conscience, if you will." The smile he gave her looked more like the Evan she knew. "I just know that I can't go on any longer knowing I've caused you such grief. And to show you I really mean it, I'm willing to sell you my half of the business."

"For a thousand dollars? You know I can't possibly come up with that amount."

"No, not a thousand." His face twisted in a wry grin. "You said the place wasn't worth more than three hundred. I'll go along with your estimate. Give me a hundred and fifty, and we'll call it even."

Jenny stared at him. "Are you serious?"

"Absolutely." He drew a folded paper from his inner coat pocket. "And to prove it, I've brought along a bill of sale."

"You mean you want to do it tonight?"

"If you have the money here at home, why not get it over with right now? Then we'll be square."

"Well, I suppose. Wait right here." She left Evan in the dark living room and carried the lamp to her bedroom, where she pulled her savings from a niche in the wall behind her bed. She sorted out a small stack of bills, then went back to Evan. "Go ahead," she told him. "Count it."

"No, I trust you." Evan pocketed the cash and scribbled his signature at the bottom of the bill of sale. "There we are, everything tied up nice and neat. I'll be going now. How about meeting me at the sheriff's office at nine?"

"Nine will be fine." She closed the door behind him and leaned against it, filled with wonder at what had just transpired. The restaurant was hers, truly hers! And tomorrow Evan would clear her name.

≥∾

The following morning, Jenny walked the familiar path to Sheriff Randolph's office by herself. No point in bothering Andrew today. She wouldn't need a protector this morning. Today was the day she would be exonerated. She strode up the steps with a confident air and rapped on the door before pushing it open.

"Is he here?" she asked the moment she set foot in the room.

Randolph looked up from behind his desk. "Is who here?"

"Evan. Evan Townsend. He said he'd meet me here at nine."

A baffled expression spread across the sheriff's face. "And why would he do that?"

"He was going to take responsibility for—" A commotion behind her made Jenny whirl around. The door burst open and Andrew appeared, pushing a stocky, balding man before him.

Jenny gasped. "Harvey Green!"

"What's going on?" Randolph demanded.

Andrew, grim-faced, shoved the man toward the sheriff. Manuel scooted into the room behind him. "Have you been looking for this man, Randolph?"

"Yes," the sheriff began, "but I want to know—"

"Good. He has something to say to you." Andrew prodded the heavyset man between his shoulder blades. "Go on. Tell them what you told Manuel and me."

Green glanced at the sheriff, then dropped his gaze to the floor. "You've got me dead to rights," he muttered. "I know I'm headed for Yuma and hard time, but I ain't going alone."

He flung his head back and stared directly at Randolph. "Townsend's going with me. He's the boss; he can take his share of the blame."

"Townsend?" Randolph echoed. "You're sure?"

Green spat on the floor. "I ought to know who gave me my orders, hadn't I? The whole thing was his idea from start to finish. The rustling, rigging those bids for the army, all of it."

"What about her?" Randolph jerked his head in Jenny's direction.

Green's lips curved in a sly smile. "That was his idea, too. He had her pay me for beef for their restaurant and the money wound up right back in his pockets. If any of this came to light, I was supposed to vamoose so she could take the blame instead of Townsend."

"So what do you think, Sheriff?" Andrew asked.

Randolph lowered his head a moment, then looked straight at Jenny. "Sounds like everything you said was true, Miss Davis. You're free to go."

Relief made Jenny's head light. She smiled her thanks at the sheriff. "I'm happy to hear that, but I'm even happier to know Evan was ready to tell you himself."

"Townsend? What do you—" The sheriff's comment was cut off when the door crashed open again. This time it was Red who entered the crowded office.

"Sheriff, I need a word with you. Andrew told me what Jenny said about Townsend being the mastermind of all these evildoings. I went to confront the man this morning, and. . ." He paused dramatically. "He's gone, Sheriff. Gone! Saddled his horse and set off for parts unknown sometime during the night."

# twenty-two

Jenny folded her dark blue dress and laid it neatly atop the others in her trunk. She reached for the dotted-Swiss, then paused to brush away the tears that filmed her eyes. Her dear house, the home she'd loved—how much it meant to her! She would leave a piece of her heart here in Tucson when she left.

It couldn't be helped, though. She heaved a shaky sigh and smoothed the dotted-Swiss out on the bed. She now carried another stain on her name. True, she had been cleared of wrongdoing in the eyes of the law, but she knew well enough that there were plenty of people who would always remember her suspected role in Evan's crimes. She couldn't go through that again.

She settled the dress in its place in the trunk. Only her smaller belongings still waited to be packed. She rested her arms on the windowsill and gazed outside. Who would tend her rosebush next summer? The thought left her even more melancholy. At least she knew the restaurant would be in good hands under Jacinta's supervision. It would bring in continued income to support the Ochoa family, and with the profits that would be sent Jenny's way, she could live comfortably wherever she went.

In a way, she looked forward to it. *I do,* she insisted, trying to stifle the voice of doubt. It would be a chance for a new start, just her and the Lord. Having time to spend getting acquainted with her Savior was the bright spot in the days ahead. Even if it meant leaving Tucson and the restaurant.

And Andrew. She stifled a sob at the thought of never seeing him again. *It's all for the best.* If only she could convince her heart of that. He would have her eternal gratitude for the way he stood by her in her darkest hour and the effort he made to clear her name. If the circumstances had been different...

"But they aren't," she said aloud. "And you might as well get used to that fact."

A knock at the door interrupted her musings. She pulled it open, expecting to find Manuel with the additional shipping crates she'd sent him after. Instead, Andrew stood on the doorstep, holding his hat in his hands. "Good morning," he said, giving her the smile that always made her knees tremble. "May I come in?"

Wordlessly, Jenny backed away from the door. Andrew entered and looked around the room, his gaze landing on the stack of boxes. He glanced back at Jenny. "What's going on?"

"I'm packing," she said, turning away to avoid his gaze. "I've decided to see what California is like."

"You're moving there? Leaving the restaurant?"

"In Jacinta's capable hands. Don't worry." She forced a laugh. "You'll still be able to enjoy her cooking."

Andrew took a step toward her. "It isn't Jacinta's cooking I'll miss." He moved nearer and took her hand. "Why leave just when God has worked everything out for you?"

Her fingers felt the tingle she always experienced whenever he touched her. "People don't forget when someone has been hauled up in front of the sheriff day after day. There'll be talk, Andrew, and lots of it. I've been through this before, and I can't do it again."

"You mean you're running away?" He brushed her cheek with the back of his hand and shook his head. "You can leave Tucson, Jenny, but you can't run away from yourself. You just carry the same problems with you from place to place. The best thing you can do is stay here, hold your head high, and keep going."

Jenny shivered at his touch. "I can't face down the rumors on my own." She raised her gaze to his face, only inches away.

"You don't have to do it alone," he murmured. "You have God—and me."

Jenny stared into Andrew's eyes, so close to hers. For the first time in her life, she didn't want to run away from a man's embrace. What would it be like to feel Andrew's lips on her own? The thought took her breath away. "I know," she whispered. "You've truly become my friend."

A low chuckle shook Andrew's chest. "I'll always be your friend. But I want to be more than that. Much more." His breath stirred the ringlets at her temple. "Don't go, Jenny. Don't leave Tucson, and more importantly, don't leave me. Won't you stay here with me. . .as my wife?"

Jenny raised her hand and pressed her fingertips against Andrew's cheek. "You know everything that's happened, and you still want to marry me?"

"More than anything in the world." He bent until his lips almost touched hers. "Will you have me?"

A wellspring of joy bubbled up inside Jenny, filling her soul until she thought she would burst. "I'll be your wife," she said, twining her arms around his neck, "and your best friend. Forever."

She raised her face to bridge the tiny gap between them. The touch of Andrew's lips on hers was everything she had longed for, and more.

# A Letter To Our Readers

Dear Reader:

In order that we might better contribute to your reading enjoyment, we would appreciate your taking a few minutes to respond to the following questions. We welcome your comments and read each form and letter we receive. When completed, please return to the following:

Fiction Editor
Heartsong Presents
PO Box 719
Uhrichsville, Ohio 44683

1. Did you enjoy reading *Refining Fire* by Carol Cox?
   ❑ Very much! I would like to see more books by this author!
   ❑ Moderately. I would have enjoyed it more if

   _____

   _____

   _____

2. Are you a member of **Heartsong Presents**? ❑ Yes ❑ No
   If no, where did you purchase this book? _____

   _____

3. How would you rate, on a scale from 1 (poor) to 5 (superior), the cover design? _____

4. On a scale from 1 (poor) to 10 (superior), please rate the following elements.

   ____ Heroine          ____ Plot
   ____ Hero             ____ Inspirational theme
   ____ Setting          ____ Secondary characters

5. These characters were special because?_____

_____

_____

6. How has this book inspired your life?_____

_____

_____

7. What settings would you like to see covered in future **Heartsong Presents** books? _____

_____

_____

8. What are some inspirational themes you would like to see treated in future books? _____

_____

_____

9. Would you be interested in reading other **Heartsong Presents** titles?  ❑ Yes  ❑ No

10. Please check your age range:

    ❑ Under 18        ❑ 18-24

    ❑ 25-34          ❑ 35-45

    ❑ 46-55          ❑ Over 55

Name_____

Occupation_____

Address_____

City_____ State_____ Zip_____

# FRONTIER BRIDES

## 4 stories in 1

**F**our romances ride through the sagebrush of yesteryear. Colleen L. Reece shares the compelling stories of people who put their lives on the line to develop a new land. . .and new love.

Historical, paperback, 464 pages, 5 ³/₁₆"x 8"

❦ ❦ ❦ ❦ ❦ ❦ ❦ ❦ ❦ ❦ ❦ ❦ ❦

❦ ❦ ❦ ❦ ❦ ❦ ❦ ❦ ❦ ❦ ❦ ❦ ❦

# Heartsong

# Presents

# $J$EARTSONG ♥ PRESENTS

# Love Stories Are Rated G!

That's for godly, gratifying, and of course, great! If you love a thrilling love story but don't appreciate the sordidness of some popular paperback romances, **Heartsong Presents** is for you. In fact, **Heartsong Presents** is the premiere inspirational romance book club featuring love stories where Christian faith is the primary ingredient in a marriage relationship.

Sign up today to receive your first set of four, never-before-published Christian romances. Send no money now; you will receive a bill with the first shipment. You may cancel at any time without obligation, and if you aren't completely satisfied with any selection, you may return the books for an immediate refund!

Imagine. . .four new romances every four weeks—two historical, two contemporary—with men and women like you who long to meet the one God has chosen as the love of their lives. . .all for the low price of $10.99 postpaid.

To join, simply complete the coupon below and mail to the address provided. **Heartsong Presents** romances are rated G for another reason: They'll arrive Godspeed!

## YES! Sign me up for Hearts♥ng!